TALONS of TIME

PAUL TWITCHELL

ECKANKAR
Minneapolis

TALONS OF TIME

Printed in U.S.A.

Compiled and adapted by Mar Amongo
from *Talons of Time* by Paul Twitchell

Illustrated by Mar Amongo

Edited by Harold Klemp and Joan Klemp

Library of Congress Cataloging-in-Publication

Amongo, Mar.
    Talons of Time / Paul Twitchell ; [compiled and adapted by Mar Amongo ; illustrated by Mar Amongo ; edited by Harold Klemp and Joan Klemp]. — Authorized ECKANKAR ed.
        p. cm.
    ISBN 1-57043-147-7 (alk. paper)
    I. Twitchell, Paul, 1908–1971. Talons of Time. II. Klemp, Harold. III. Klemp, Joan. IV. Title.
PN6727.A428T35 1999
741.5'973—dc21   99-13511
                                                         CIP

Authorized ECKANKAR edition.

∞ The paper used in this publication meets the minimum requirements of the American National Standard for Information Sciences—Permanence of Paper for Printed Library Materials, ANSI Z39.48-1984.

The TALONS of TIME

NOTHING EXISTS, BECAUSE NOTHING IS. ONLY THE SUGMAD IS ALL, AND ALL IS THE **SUGMAD.**

TIME IS ONLY A RIVER OF PARTICLES MOVING THROUGH SPACE. IT IS NOT THE FRAME OF THE WORLD OF NATURE BUT THE WORLD OF OUR OWN SENSE PERCEPTIONS. TIME CANNOT EXIST WITHOUT AN OBSERVER, AND WHAT IS SEEN AS OBJECTIVE TIME DOES NOT EXIST AT ALL.

I KNOW THIS AFTER MY TERRIBLE EXPERIENCE WITH THOSE STRANGE BEINGS KNOWN AS THE *TIME MAKERS.* I REALIZED THAT I WAS VIEWING AN AWFUL CRIME UPON HUMANITY BY THOSE TERRIBLE CREATURES, TO SUBDUE IT TO THEIR OWN WILL.

I WAS COMING HOME LATE, AN ALL-EVENING DIALOGUE ON *ECKANKAR,* THE ANCIENT SCIENCE OF SOUL TRAVEL.

AWOOOOONNGG

TOK TOK TOK

THE BEAUTY OF THAT OCTOBER NIGHT THRILLED ME WITH THE SUBTLE MYSTERY OF ECK, AS MY FOOTSTEPS ECHOED IN THE NIGHT, COMPETING WITH THE DISTANT BAYING OF THE HOUNDS AND THE SOUNDS OF THE NIGHT INSECTS. THEN I MET OLLIE.

MR. SKALLY'S BEEN LOOKING FOR YOU. HE ASKED IF I SAW YOU ANYWHERE TO TELL YOU TO COME BY HIS HOUSE REGARDLESS OF THE TIME.

HOW LONG AGO WAS THIS?

OLLIE RELATED HOW JOHN SKALLY WAS VERY UPSET OVER SOMETHING. THEN HE BADE ME GOOD NIGHT.

JOHN SKALLY NEVER GETS EXCITED. IT MUST BE SOMETHING VERY IMPORTANT.

JOHN SKALLY WAS ONE OF THE LEADING SCIENTISTS OF THE MODERN AGE, WORKING ON A SECRET PROJECT CONCERNING TIME FOR **FORT AIR INDUSTRY.**

HE'S PECULIAR AS A GENIUS. BUT HE NEVER GETS EXCITED.

I WALKED TOWARD THE TOWN COMMONS THINKING OF JOHN SKALLY, THEN UPON REACHING HIS GEORGIAN-STYLE HOUSE...

THERE'S A LIGHT INSIDE THE HOUSE.

2

I RAPPED SEVERAL TIMES ON THE DOOR, BUT GETTING NO RESPONSE I WENT TO THE SIDE OF THE HOUSE AND PEERED THROUGH THE STUDY WINDOW.

HIS LEATHER BOOKS APPEAR TO BE THE SAME. BUT THAT FISHBOWL IS BLAZING IN WILD COLORS.

BESIDES THE FISH, I NOTICED THAT TEDDY, THE WATCHDOG, DIDN'T CHALLENGE ME. I MOVED TO THE BACK OF THE HOUSE LOOKING LIKE A THIEF TRYING TO SLIP INSIDE.

MY MEMORY OF THE PAST WITH JOHN SKALLY FORCED ITSELF UPON MY MIND. HE IS MY BEST FRIEND, WHO HELPED ME GET A JOB ON THE NEWSPAPER WHEN MY PARENTS DIED. SINCE HE BEGAN TO WORK ON A SPECIAL PROJECT CONCERNING TIME, HE GREW THINNER AND ACTED AS THOUGH HE WERE IN A TRANCE ALL THE TIME.

STRANGE CULTS, SPACE PHENOMENA, OCCULT GROUPS, AND PSYCHIC INVESTIGATION FRIGHTEN THE AVERAGE PERSON, WHO DOES NOT HAVE THE KNOWLEDGE OF ECK.

I KNOW, BUT YOU YOURSELF KNOW MUCH ABOUT ECKANKAR.

MY THOUGHTS WERE INTERRUPTED, AND I PROCEEDED TO LOOK AROUND THE HOUSE.

WHAT HAS HAPPENED? I CAN'T UNDERSTAND WHAT'S GOING ON!

3

I CROSSED TO THE DESK AND LOOKED AT THE NOTEBOOK.

THE WORDS FROM HIS NOTEBOOK LEAPED OUT AT ME TELLING A STORY OF HIS TIME SPENT WITH THE **TIME MAKERS**, HOW TERRIBLE THEY WERE AND HOW THEY KEPT THE SECRET OF TIME FROM THE EARTH PEOPLE.

THE STORY REVEALED HIS DEEP INVOLVEMENT IN THE STUDY OF TIME, HOW HE REVILED SCIENCES AND PHILOSO-PHIES WHICH NEVER GAVE THOUGHT TO TIME BEING ONE OF THE GREATEST OF THE GENERAL PROPERTIES EXHIBITED BY MASS BODIES.

TIME AND **SPACE** HAD BEEN PUT ON THE SAME LEVEL AND TREATED AS EQUAL.

IN THEIR THEORY, **TIME AND SPACE BE-CAME COUNTEPARTS** WHICH IS NOT TRUE. THIS IS WRONG FOR WHEN I EVOKE TIME, IT IS **SPACE THAT ANSWERS THE CALL**, JOHN SKALLY REVEALED.

TIME IS SAID TO BE VERY ELUSIVE. WE ENCOUNTER IT IN EVERYTHING WE DO AND OBSERVE, AND IN OUR VERY ACT OF EXAMINATION IT ESCAPES US FOR IT IS NO LONGER PRESENT BUT PAST.

TIME LIKE SPACE BECOMES A PROBLEM WITH THE SCIENTIFIC MIND BUT I FOUND THE ANSWER A LONG TIME AGO AS A PRISONER IN THE LAND OF THE TWO-HEADED GOD. THE TIME MAKERS ARE RESPONSIBLE FOR THE ILLUSION OF GROWTH AND AGING. THEY ARE THE **ORIGINATORS OF TIME**. THEY CREATED THE **TRAP OF MAYA**.

5

THE TIME MAKERS ENSLAVED THE MATERIAL WORLD WITH ILLUSORY TRAPS. BUT SKALLY LEARNED THAT TIME IS ONLY DURATION WHICH IMPLIES EXISTENCE.

BUT DURATION AND EXISTENCE ARE NOT IDENTICAL. WHILE IT IS TRUE THAT DURATION IMPLIES EXISTENCE THE REVERSE IS NOT TRUE, FOR EXISTENCE DOES NOT IMPLY DURATION.

DURATION IS A CONTINUED EXISTENCE. IT SIMPLY MEANS THE PERSISTENCE OF A BEING IN EXISTENCE.

KAL NIRANJAN, THE TWO-HEADED GOD OF SUKHSHAM PAD, OFTEN CALLED TURIYA PAD, IS IN COMPLETE AND SIMULTANEOUS POSSESSION OF ENDLESS LIFE. HE IS WITHOUT BEGINNING OR END, WITHOUT CHANGE OR SEQUENCE, WITHOUT PAST OR FUTURE.

HE EXISTS BECAUSE IT IS NECESSARY. HE LIVES AND ACTS IN LIMITLESS FULNESS, WITHOUT DECREASE OR INCREASE, IN AN EVERLASTING PRESENT.

THE TIME MAKERS DO NOT CONSIST OF MATERIAL PARTS AND FORM. NO MATERIAL COMPOUNDS, THEY LIVE DIFFRENTLY FROM THAT OF THE PHYSICAL BODIES. THEY HAVE A NATURAL EXISTENCE WHICH, THOUGH IT HAD BEGINNING, HAS NO END.

6

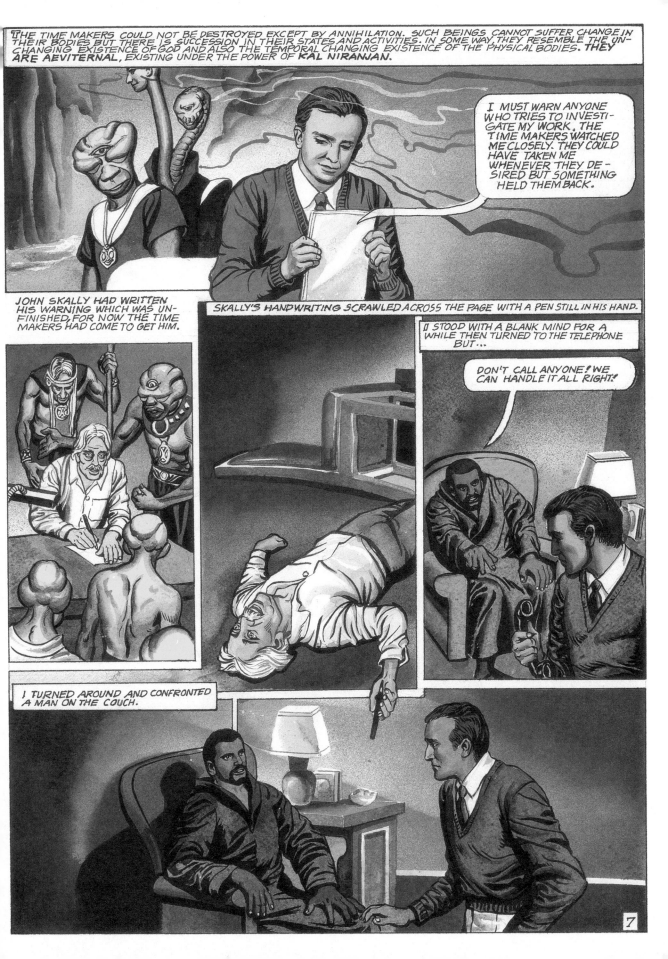

THE MAN INTRODUCED HIMSELF AS SHARIR. HE WAS ASKING ME TO ASSIST IN RECOVERING JOHN SKALLY'S TUZA, WHICH IS THE SOUL OF THE INDIVIDUAL, IN SUKHSHAM PAD.

JOHN SKALLY THE BODY WAS DEAD BUT HIS TUZA LIVES ON UNTIL KAL NIRANJAN DECIDES TO ANNIHILATE HIM COMPLETELY, SHARIR TOLD ME.

IT IS YOUR DUTY TO BE ONE OF US. WE WILL RESCUE HIM FROM THE FATE THAT AWAITS THE WHOLE WORLD.

WHAT CAN WE DO? HE IS ALREADY DEAD.

HE WILL NOT EVEN BE A VIEWPOINT IN THE WORLD OF INVISIBILITY. THINK OF THAT, THE GREAT MIND OF JOHN SKALLY WILL COMPLETELY BE DEAD.

I DIDN'T COMPLETELY TRUST THE STRANGER BUT THE KEY TO THE MYSTERY MIGHT BE IN HIS HANDS. I LEARNED FROM HIM THAT JOHN SKALLY HAD BEEN CAPTURED IN THE PAST BUT HIS KNOWLEDGE ABOUT THE SECRET OF TIME BECAME TOO GREAT A THREAT TO SUKHSHAM PAD.

MAN KNOWS SO LITTLE ABOUT TIME. THEN, WE ASK OURSELVES WHAT IS THIS MYSTERIOUS CONTRADICTION CALLED TIME?

I STARED AT SHARIR BLANKLY, THEN A DEADLY SILENCE HOVERED ABOUT THE HOUSE AND I FELT SOMETHING WAS READY TO SNATCH ME INTO THE FAR UNKNOWN.

THAT IS EXACTLY WHAT WE, THE MAGICIANS OF LO, WANT TO KNOW.

WHATEVER SECRET MIGHT BE IS CONTAINED IN JOHN'S SECRET DIARY. WHETHER OR NOT WE FIND IT, WE MUST STILL GO AFTER JOHN SKALLY TO SAVE HIM FROM COMPLETE DESTRUCTION!

I HURRIEDLY CAME DOWN THE THE LADDER BESIDE HIM.

THE FISH IN THE JAR LOOKED DEAD. I PANICKED. DEADLY SILENCE HAD SUDDENLY GROWN. THE SILENCE DROPPED UPON THE HOUSE LIKE A CURTAIN FALLING—STOPPING EVERYTHING, INCLUDING OUR BREATHING.

THE HUSH CAUGHT ME AND I WAS WEAKENED AND IMMO-BILE. SHARIR WAS STANDING AS THOUGH SUSPENDED IN THE AIR.

A STRANGE SIGH LIKE A FAINT WIND GOT INTO MY FLESH—AND TWISTED LIKE A KNIFE.

TIME HAD NO EFFECT ON THE ATMA SARUP AND SO SHARIR AND I WERE ABLE TO COMMUNICATE WITH EACH OTHER.

DO EXACTLY AS I TELL YOU AND THERE WILL BE NO DANGER.

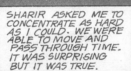
SHARIR ASKED ME TO CONCENTRATE AS HARD AS I COULD. WE WERE ABLE TO MOVE AND PASS THROUGH TIME. IT WAS SURPRISING BUT IT WAS TRUE.

WE EMERGED FROM THE KITCHEN AND EVERY-THING WAS FIXED IN TIME AROUND THE HOUSE.

WE KNOW BETTER. WE ARE ABLE TO RETAIN OUR CONSCIOUSNESS AND CAST OFF THE SPELL. THIS IS ONE WAY OF DEFEATING THE TIME MAKERS.

SHARIR TOLD ME THE TIME MAKERS HAD THROWN A NET OVER THE HOUSE WHICH CAUGHT US IMMOBILE. WE WERE ABLE TO BREAK THROUGH IT. HE ASSURED ME WE COULD ELUDE THEM.

SHARIR BROKE MY SILENCE

WE WILL GO TO SEE MR. HARRY GLAZER, THE PUBLISHER OF THE NEWSPAPER YOU'RE WORKING WITH.

HARRY GLAZER BUT WHAT HAS HE GOT TO DO WITH ALL THIS?

WE WALKED ACROSS THE TOWN COMMONS TO THE OTHERSIDE OF THE CITY. THE NEWSPAPER BUILDING WAS WELL LIT. SHARIR PUNCHED THE DOOR BELL SEVERAL TIMES UNTIL THE JANITOR PEERED THROUGH THE CRACK, BUT WENT BACK INSIDE. MINUTES LATER, HE OPENED THE DOOR. WE RODE THE ELEVATOR TO THE THIRD FLOOR.

AH... I MIGHT HAVE KNOWN THAT YOU WOULD BE HERE IN TIME OF TROUBLE!

YOU WILL LEARN SOON ENOUGH.

EXCITED BUT CAUTIOUS, GLAZER LED US INSIDE HIS OFFICE.

SHARIR EXPLAINED WHAT HAD HAPPENED TO JOHN SKALLY.

I HOPE THAT SOME OF MY PEOPLE HAVE GOTTEN THERE BY NOW. THEY HADN'T WHEN WE LEFT.

12

SHARIR WANTED THE BODY OF SKALLY PRESERVED UNTIL THE TUZA WAS GOTTEN BACK INTO HIS BODY AGAIN. THIS WAS NECESSARY TO AVOID ANY TROUBLE WITH THE PEOPLE. HE ASKED GLAZER NOT TO PRINT IN HIS NEWSPAPER ANYTHING ABOUT THE INCIDENT WHICH MIGHT ALARM THE PEOPLE OF THE WORLD.

I WILL TAKE CARE OF THE POLICE AND NOTHING WILL BE PRINTED. I PROMISE YOU THAT.

THROUGH THE WINDOW OF THE PUBLISHING HOUSE, I COULD SEE THE LITTLE CITY TWINKLING UNDER THE MOON. THIS WAS HARRY GLAZER'S WORLD, A SMALL EMPIRE THAT COVERED THIS LITTLE VALLEY WHILE THE STRUGGLE FOR THE WHOLE UNIVERSE WAS QUIETLY TAKING PLACE.

HARRY GLAZER WAS A MAN OF WEALTH, SPENDING MOST OF HIS FORTY YEARS IN MANY BUSINESSES. HE ASSURED ME THAT MY PAY WOULD CONTINUE UNTIL THE DURATION OF MY RETURN TO EARTH WITH SHARIR.

SKALLY'S KNOWLEDGE ABOUT TIME ENORMOUSLY LIFTED MANKIND, BUT THE STRUGGLE BETWEEN SUKHSHAM AND THE UNIVERSE HAD GROWN. BUT FEW IN SCIENCE KNEW IT AND PERHAPS JOHN SKALLY WAS THE ONLY MAN IN THE WORLD WHO KNEW THIS.

THAT DIARY IS MORE IMPORTANT THAN SKALLY. IT MEANS THE SURVIVAL OF THIS UNIVERSE. IF IT IS LOST, THEN EVERYTHING IS GONE.

AS A RESULT OF JOHN SKALLY'S STRUGGLE AGAINST THE TIME MAKERS, FOR THE SURVIVAL OF MANKIND, HIS LIFE BECAME TERRIFYING.

13

IT INFLUENCED PEOPLE LIKE YOU, HARRY, PEDDAR, AND MYSELF BECAUSE HE COULD NOT TAKE MANY INTO HIS CONFIDENCE. HE HAD TO DO IT PRACTICALLY ALONE.

'HE COULD NOT TRUST ANYONE, NOT EVEN HIMSELF. IN THIS CENTURY, EVERYTHING IS CRACKING UP, EVERYTHING IS ISOLATED UNLESS WE CAN SAVE IT NOW,' SHARIR EXPLAINED FURTHER.

DO YOU WANT ME TO CHECK ON JOHN SKALLY'S BODY? I CAN SEND ONE OF MY MEN OUT THERE.

SHARIR ASKED GLAZER TO WAIT UNTIL HE COULD CHECK WITH THE PEOPLE IN THE MONASTERY OF LO. THEN HE WENT TO THE RADIO ROOM AND USED THE SHORT WAVE. GLAZER TURNED TO ME.

YOU HAVE GIVEN ME AN ASSIGNMENT IN ETERNITY!

BRING ME BACK A GOOD STORY, BUT IT WON'T BE PRINTED.

HARRY GLAZER'S ENTHUSIASM IN SENDING ME TO SUKHSHAM PAD WAS SO STRONG BUT I WAS DOUBTFUL ABOUT TRAVELING THROUGH THE BARRIER OF TIME.

HE ASKED ME TO TRUST SHARIR AS HIS GRANDFATHER AND HIS FATHER HAD. HE REVEALED TO ME THAT SHARIR WAS AGE-LESS AND ASSURED ME THAT THE JOURNEY WOULD BE A GREAT ADVENTURE.

SHARIR CAME BACK INTO THE ROOM AND INFORMED US THAT SKALLY'S BODY WAS BEING TAKEN CARE OF AT THE MONASTERY OF LO. GLAZER SOON LED US OUT OF THE ROOM.

IS IT POSSIBLE THAT A HARD-BOILED EDITOR IN CHIEF WHO DRIVES HIS EDITORIAL STAFF TO DESPAIR HAS CHANGED HEART? AND IS IT POS-SIBLE I COULD LIVE A HUNDRED YEARS WITHOUT AGING?

I READ EINSTEIN'S THEORY AND OTHER SYSTEMS BUT NO-THING MADE MUCH SENSE!

14

WE STOPPED AT A SMALL ROOM WITHOUT ANY WINDOWS. GLAZER PROMISED ME A PENSION TO BE GIVEN BY HIS HEIRS ONCE I GOT BACK TO EARTH AFTER A HUNDRED YEARS.

IF I CAN GET THROUGH THE AGE BARRIER, I'LL BE WAITING FOR YOU, PEDDAR.

WE SHOOK HANDS AGAIN. HE PRESSED A SMALL BUTTON HIDDEN IN THE WALL, AND THE DOOR OPENED.

SHARIR LED THE WAY AS THOUGH HE HAD BEEN HERE MANY TIMES.

WE ENTERED IT AND WENT DOWN INTO THE TUNNEL.

I FELT HEMMED IN, SUFFOCATING FROM THE NARROWNESS OF THE PASSAGEWAY. I THOUGHT OF BEING BURIED ALIVE. SHARIR NOTICED THIS AND PROMISED TO CURE ME OF THIS CLAUSTROPHOBIA.

FROM SHARIR, I'D LEARNED ALSO HOW GLAZER'S FATHER BECAME A MEMBER OF THE CLOSELY GUARDED BROTHERHOOD IN THE MONASTERY OF LO, OF HOW SYSTEMATICALLY HE WAS TAUGHT THE FUNDAMENTAL LAWS USEFUL TO HIS TIME.

THREE GENERATIONS OF GLAZIER'S FAMILY WERE TRAINED IN THE MYSTERY SCIENCES AND WE'VE FOUND HARRY VERY USEFUL IN HELPING MANKIND DEFEAT THE TIME MAKERS.

15

WE STOPPED FOR A WHILE, THEN WALKED AGAIN FOR ANOTHER HALF HOUR UNTIL WE REACHED A HUGE DOOR PAINTED WITH ORIENTAL DESIGNS.

WE ARE HERE!

HE PUSHED THE DOOR OPEN AND I STARED IN AMAZEMENT AT THE SIGHT.

THE GIGANTIC ROOM APPEARED TO BE A HANGAR FILLED WITH SPACESHIPS. SHARIR AND I WALKED ACROSS IT.

THE TALL CAPTAIN BLOPTER GREETED US AND TOLD US THAT THE SHIP WAS BEING READIED FOR THE JOURNEY, THEN SHOWED US A HUGE MAP.

YOU'LL HAVE PLENTY OF EXCITEMENT ALL RIGHT. THAT IS WHERE YOU'RE GOING.

MY HEART POUNDED WITH EXCITEMENT AND I COULD NOT HIDE MY FEELINGS ON THIS.

WHAT AN AMOUNT OF SPACE!

SPACE IS VERY DIFFERENT FROM TIME.

16

PLATO WAS ONE OF THE FIRST TO TEACH THAT THIS UNIVERSE WAS A TRAP FOR SOUL, BECAUSE ITS OPPOSED TO SPIRIT BEINGS. THIS PROBABLY MEANT HE WAS HITTING ON THE TRUTH THAT THIS UNIVERSE ISN'T SUITABLE FOR MAN, BECAUSE OF THE ELEMENT CALLED **TIME.**

THIS WORLD IS A WORLD OF GROWTH FOR THINGS OF MATTER COMING TO LIFE. THIS IS WHY SOUL MUST DEVELOP A FLESHY BODY TO LIVE IN IT. MOTION AND CHANGE ARE PARTS OF LIFE. ITS NATURAL ELEMENTS COMBINE TO FORM COMPOUNDS THEN DISSOLVE TO FORM OTHER COMPOUNDS.

THIS COMBINATION AND RECOMBINATION GO ON UNINTERRUPTEDLY, SHARIR REVEALED. BODIES DO NOT MOVE THROUGH TIME BUT THROUGH DEFINITE REGIONS OF SPACE. TIME IS THE FORCE THAT MOVES THROUGH THINGS UPON THIS UNIVERSE. TIME IS MOTION. WITHOUT TIME THERE WOULD BE NO MOTION. THIS IS THE **GREAT TRAP OF THE TIME MAKERS.**

THEY LURE SOULS INTO THIS UNIVERSE AND TRAP THEM HERE AND MAKE THEM BELIEVE THAT THIS IS THE **GARDEN OF EDEN,** AND WHEN THEY AWAKEN TO THE TRUTH, IT IS TOO LATE.

IF IT WERE NOT FOR THE **MAGICIANS OF LO AND THEIR ASSOCIATES,** LIKE **GLAZER** AND **SKALLY,** PLACED UPON THIS EARTH TO CONTINUALLY FIGHT **KAL NIRANJAN** AND THE **TIME MAKERS,** TIME OR MOTION WOULD STOP AND LIFE WOULD COME TO A HALT.

ACCORDING TO SHARIR, THIS WAS IMPOSSIBLE NOW BUT EVENTUALLY WOULD BE. THEY WERE TRYING TO EDUCATE PEOPLE DESPITE THE SETBACK RECEIVED FROM THE AGENTS OF **KAL NIRANJAN** AMONG PEOPLE.

WHY DON'T YOU MOVE PEOPLE OF THIS UNIVERSE INTO ANOTHER ONE WHERE TIME WOULD NOT AFFECT THEM?

IN ORDER TO LEAD THEM ASTRAY, THEY ARE MADE TO BELIEVE THAT KAL IS THE GOD OF ALL CREATION AND EARTH IS THEIR NATURAL HABITAT.

17

THE WALL PHONE JIN-GLED, AND CAPTAIN BLOPTER ANNOUNCED THAT THE SHIP WAS ALMOST READY. MOMENTS LATER WE WERE DIRECT-ED TO ANOTHER ROOM.

UPON HIS TOUCH THE DOOR SWUNG OPEN.

WE PUT ON THE SPACE SUITS AND WAITED, BUT I SUFFERED THE AGONY OF THE PRESSURE CHAMBER.

I FELT NERVOUS AND FRIGHTENED AND SHARIR CALMED ME, FOR IN A SHORT TIME I WOULD ADJUST TO THE CLIMATE OF SPACE. THE DOOR OPENED AND WE WALKED TO THE WAITING SHIP.

THIS IS NECESSARY FOR TRAVELING THROUGH SPACE WHILE STILL IN THE PHYSICAL BODY. BUT AFTER WE CROSS THE BORDERS INTO THE **LAND OF SUKHSHAM PAD,** WE WILL BE TRAVELING IN THE **NURI SARUP,** OR THE LIGHT BODY.

WE ENTERED THE BOWEL OF THE SHIP WHICH WAS LONG AND NAR-ROW, AND ITS CEILING REACHED UP TO FIFTY FEET.

SITTING THERE GAVE ME A FEELING OF VERTIGO. I WANTED TO LEAP FOR THE DOOR THAT WAS CLOSING BEHIND US. MY MIND COULD ONLY SEE DARKNESS, BUT CAPTAIN BLOPTER TOUCHED MY SHOULDER AND THIS DROVE AWAY MY ANGUISH..

18

THE SHIP TREMBLED AS THE ENGINE STARTED, AND THROUGH THE PORT-HOLE I COULD SEE THE EARTH FALLING AWAY.

MY VERTIGO RETURNED AGAIN BUT THIS TIME SHARIR HYPNO-TIZED ME **AND OVERPOWERED** ME WITH A SOOTHING WARMTH THAT PUT ME TO SLEEP FOR AN HOUR. I WOKE UP AND THE CABIN BOY PUT ME INTO A BUNK.

I ROSE FROM THE BED AND FELT HUNGRY, AND I WAS LED INTO THE DINING ROOM.

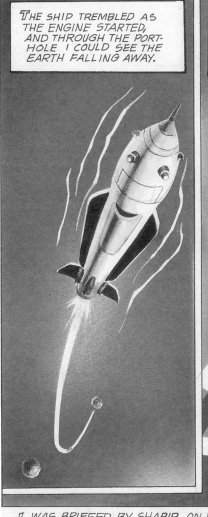

YOU FEELING BETTER?

I WAS BRIEFED BY *SHARIR* ON WHAT TO EXPECT UPON ENTERING THE PLANET OF ARCTURUS. THE ATMOSPHERE AROUND IT WOULD HAVE LESS OXYGEN, MAKING BREATHING DIFFICULT AND PAINFUL AT FIRST, BUT WHEN THE LUNGS ADJUSTED TO IT, ALL WOULD BECOME NORMAL. BECAUSE OF THE LACK OF GRAVITY, MOVEMENT WOULD EITHER BE BY WALKING OR FLOATING IN THE AIR.

WHEN I QUESTIONED SHARIR ABOUT THE GOVERNMENT OF SUKHSHAM, HE EXPLAINED THAT SUKHSHAM WAS LIKE ANY COUNTRY OF THE WORLD. IT HAD ARMIES TOO, BUT THIS COUNTRY WAS ENCIRCLED BY A **PSYCHIC FENCE** AND ANY INTRUDERS WERE DEALT WITH SWIFTLY. I FELT A PAIN OF FEAR IN MY STOMACH. WE THEN PROCEEDED TO THE MAIN CHAMBER.

BETTER TAKE A SEAT AND GET STRAPPED DOWN. WE'LL BE COMING INTO THE PORT WITHIN THE NEXT HALF HOUR.

19

AFTER WE STRAPPED OURSELVES INTO THE CHAIRS, THE SHIP RUMBLED AND WALLOWED AND DIPPED STEEPLY, AND CONFUSED PATTERNS OF OBJECTS CROSSED THE SCREEN. FINALLY IT SETTLED AND CAPTAIN BLOPTER STOOD.

WECOME TO ARCTURUS GENTLEMEN!

THE SHIP'S DOOR OPENED. I FLOATED OUT THE DOOR AND GASPED FOR BREATH.

I FEEL GIDDY!

DOUBTS POUNDED IN MY HEAD, I BEGAN TO THINK THE MISSION OF SHARIR WOULD END AMONG HOSTILES.

I HOPE THIS IS NOT A TRAP.

THE CAPTAIN LAUGHED BUT IT WAS A CRUEL LAUGHTER.

SHARIR HAILED A TAXI, BUT THE ROBOT AT THE CONTROL GAVE ME AN UNPLEASANT EMOTIONAL REACTION.

THE TAXI FLEW OVER RAMBLING TAWDRY STRUCTURES SO STRANGE, MADE MORE FANTASTIC BY THE DOUBLE REDDISH SUNS.

ROWS AND ROWS OF PARKED AIRSHIPS IN THE AIRFIELD GLISTENED IN THE REDDISH LIGHT. THE COUNTRY LOOKED AGELESS MADE MORE MYSTICAL BY THE DOUBLE SUNS MOVING TOWARD ONE ANOTHER.

SHARIR BROKE MY INWARD INQUIRY BY CAUTIONING ME TO KEEP OUR JOURNEY TO THE HEADQUARTERS IN COMPLETE SECRECY.

WE SKIRTED THE LAKE AND LOOKED DOWN AT THE DWELLINGS SQUATTED ALONG IT.

THIS WORLD LOOKS VERY PEACEFUL.

BY THEIR NEARNESS TO SUKHSHAM, THEIR PSYCHIC POWERS ARE GREATER THAN EARTH PEOPLE AND NATURALLY MORE PEACEFUL, BUT DON'T BE MISTAKEN BY THE ABILITY OF THE ARCTURIANS TO DEFEND THEMSELVES WHEN ATTACKED.

THEIR GOVERNMENT HAS GREAT ARMIES.

WE PASSED ACROSS A PLATEAU OF TREES AND LANDED NEAR A GREAT CASTLE.

WE ENTERED THE CASTLE PASSING ARCTURIAN GUARDS WHO SALUTED SHARIR. WE WENT INTO THE INTERIOR OF THE CASTLE AND **EPISCOPOS**, THE COMMANDER OF THE **ARCTURIAN INTELLIGENCE**, MET US. AFTER OBTAINING HIS PERMISSION TO HELP US TAKE CARE OF OUR BODIES WHILE ON OUR WAY TO **THE PAOSHAN MOUNTAINS**, SHARIR INTRODUCED ME AS DISCIPLE OF MASTER REBAZAR TARZS.

WE WILL TAKE CARE OF YOUR BODIES BUT BEWARE OF THE **TIGER OF THE ZODIAC**, PROBABLY YOUR FIRST MENACE. YES, WE WILL HELP YOU BUT KEEP OUR GOVERNMENT OUT OF THE PICTURE. I KNOW THE MASTER'S CONTRIBUTION TO MANKIND.

KAL NIRANJAN HAS PLACED THE **TIGER** TO GUARD THAT PORTION OF THE FRONTIER. MANY OF OUR PEOPLE HAVE DISAPPEARED THERE AND THEIR BONES FOUND YEARS LATER.

BUT FAR MORE DANGEROUS IS THE **MATE OF THE TIGER.**

SHE WILL CHARM YOU AND LURE YOU TO YOUR DEATH!

SHE?

SHE IS IN A WOMAN'S FORM. THE WOMAN IS MOST DANGEROUS TO MAN. SHE WILL MAKE YOU FALL IN LOVE WITH HER, THEN YOU ARE AT HER MERCY. YOU BECOME HER SLAVE, DESIRING HER CONSTANTLY.

AND HE WHO DESIRES KNOWS THE SOURCE OF ALL PAIN. I WARNED YOU, SO LET'S GO ON WITH THE JOURNEY.

EPISCOPOS ASSIGNED A SPACE CAR TO CARRY US TO THE **PAOSHAN MOUNTAINS.** IT WAS THE WILDEST AREA IN THE UNIVERSE.

THE QUESTION AS TO WHO WAS THE GREATER DANGER TO MEN KEPT ME DEEPLY IN THOUGHT, BUT SHARIR SAID THAT THE **TALONS OF TIME** IS A GREATER THREAT TO MAN THAN THIS MATE OF THE TIGER.

WE ARE NOT CERTAIN WHAT THIS DANGER IS EXCEPT THAT IT TRAPS THE SOUL AND FIXES IT IN TIME.

22

SHARIR PROMISED TO UNLOCK THE KEY TO THE DIARY FROM MY MIND ONCE WE GOT TO THE PAOSHAN HEAD-QUARTERS.

EVEN IF THE TIME MAKERS HAVE IT, WE STILL HAVE TO GET JOHN SKALLY OUT OF SUKHSHAM PAD.

SUDDENLY, I BECAME AWARE OF THE SHIP TAKING A DIP INTO THE GORGE, AND THE SPACE-CAR SPEEDING BESIDE AND ABOVE THE PAOSHAN MOUNTAINS.

I SAW THE MOUNTAIN FALL AWAY SHARPLY. THE SHIP WAS PUTTING SWIFTLY DOWN TO A DANGEROUS LANDING ON THE VERY EDGE OF THE CRAG.

THEN WE SIGHTED THE WAY STATION PERCHED HIGH ON A STEEP CRAG OF THE MOUNTAIN.

THERE IT IS!

BRAMM

AFTER THE QUICK LANDING, THREE HOODED FIGURES MET US AGAINST THE WHIPPING WIND.

KJOOOOOOOO

23

WELCOME TO OUR REMOTE REFUGE. I AM TA SHAN, THE HEAD OF THIS STATION. COME, WE WILL FEED YOU AND ATTEND TO YOUR NEEDS.

WE STRUGGLED UP THE SLOPE TOWARD THE BATTERED BUILDING.

TA SHAN PUSHED THE DOOR AND I PERCEIVED FIGURES THAT APPEARED TO BE NURSES WORKING OVER SHADDOWED FIGURES.

YOU NEED NOT BE NERVOUS. WE ARE BUSY RESTORING TUZAS INTO THEIR ORIGINAL BODIES OR VICE VERSA AS THEY COME AND GO ACROSS THE BORDERS OF SUKHSHAM.

I TOOK AN EMPTY COT TO STRETCH MY STIFF MUSCLES BUT COULD NOT RELAX. AN EERIE SILENCE STIRRED, OVERWHELMING THE WIND BATTERING THE WALL. I SENSE A LOW DEEP HUMMING CREEPING FROM BEYOND THE LAND OF SUKHSHAM PAD.

HUMMMMM

SUDDENLY A DEEP AND BOTTOMLESS PIT OF SLEEP OVERCAME ME. MY LIFE AND EVERYTHING I KNEW WERE GONE WHEN I WOKE UP I HAD NO BODY BUT WHITE LIGHT, LIGHT CIRCLING AROUND ME.

I WAS ALARMED. I COULD SEE FROM ALL ANGLES, AND WHEN I CRIED OUT ALL TONGUES CAME FROM ME.

24

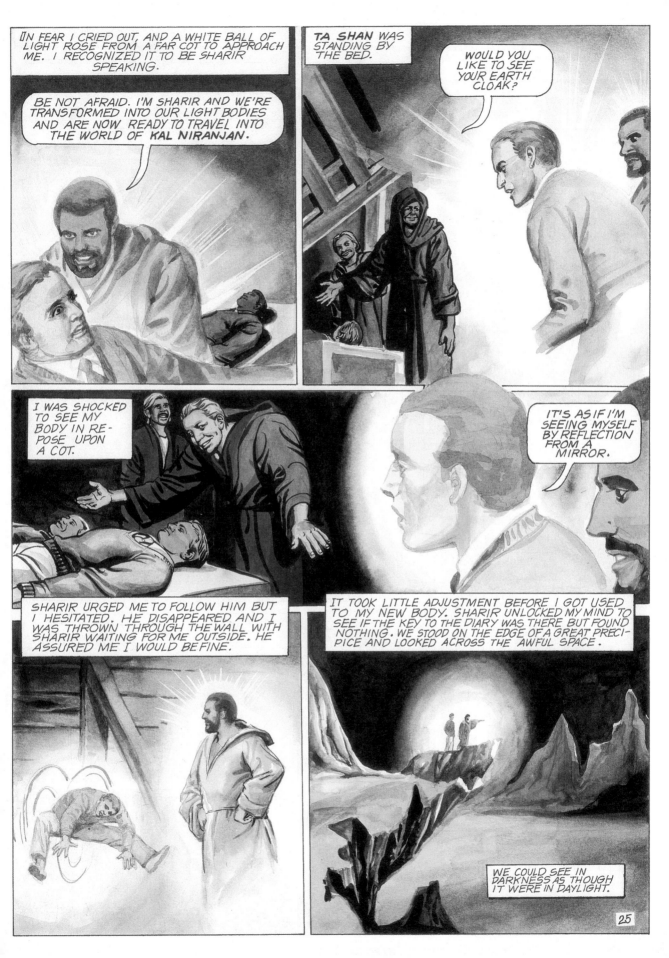

FROM WHERE WE STOOD, WE COULD SEE A SHELF THAT OPENED INTO THE MOUNTAIN. BEYOND WAS THE **VALLEY OF GIRGENTI**, THE ROUTE TO FOLLOW INTO SUKHSHAM.

YOU CAN WALK IN SPACE AS WELL AS ON THE GROUND. LOOK CLOSELY— THE PSYCHIC FENCE.

THE INHABITANTS OF SUKHSHAM WHEN READY TO GIVE UP THEIR BODIES ARE TRANSPORTED TO A HIGHER WORLD CALLED **TIRKUTI**, BUT THEY ARE NOT SENT AWAY EXCEPT WHEN THEIR KNOWLEDGE BECOMES TOO GREAT FOR THE **KAL**.

A STRANGE SET OF FLICKERING LIGHTS, SLIDING LIKE DANCING FIRE FROM ONE END OF THE UNIVERSE TO THE OTHER, CAME INTO FOCUS.

WE COULD CROSS **THE BAND OF TIME** TO REACH THE VALLEY OF GIRGENTI AND BEYOND IT **THE RIVER OF DEATH**. SHARIR SAID THAT THIS UNIVERSE HAD NO TIME AND ONE COULD LIVE LONG WITHOUT AGING. IT IS CALLED **THE FOURTH DIMENSION**.

THAT PLACE IS ONE OF THE LOOPHOLES THROUGH WHICH THE **SMUGGLERS** OF THE TWO WORLDS WORK.

BUT NOT TOO MANY COULD GO THERE BECAUSE **KAL NIRANJAN IS A LOVER OF EVIL** AND THOSE WHO GATHER AROUND HIM ARE LOVERS OF HIS PHILOSOPHY.

NOW, I THINK WE SHOULD CROSS THE BAND OF TIME.

WE FLEW ACROSS THE BAND OF TIME TOWARD THE FLAMING FIRE BUT A GIGANTIC CLIFF BLOCKED US. SHARIR SEARCHED AMONG THE BOULDERS UNTIL HE FOUND THE MOUTH OF A LARGE CAVE. WITH OUR BODIES LIGHTING THE GLOOMY CAVERN OF DRIPPING STALACTITES, WE WENT ON FOR A LONG DISTANCE.

AFTER AN ASCENT, WE CAME OUT INTO THE WIDE WINDY DARKNESS AND VIEWED TWO GIGANTIC MOUNTAINS RISING HIGH AGAINST THE DARK SKY.

THIS TIME SHARIR CAUTIONED ME NOT TO TALK UNTIL HE SAID SO. WE ONLY COMMUNICATED WITH OUR THOUGHTS. THE LIGHT OF OUR BODIES WENT OUT INSTANTLY. I COULD ONLY SEE THAT FAINT OUTLINE OF HIS FORM. SUDDENLY...

DID YOU HEAR THAT?

HEAR WHAT?

SHISSSSS

I TURNED MY LEFT SIDE INTO THE WIND AND HEARD A STRANGE MOANING IN THE WIND, WHICH TURNED INTO A BELLOWING RAGE.

GGRRLLLLL

THE TIGER!

YES. WE MUST CHANGE OUR COURSE OVER TO THE MOUNTAIN. ITS LAIR IS NEAR THE HEAD OF THE VALLEY!

I SENSED THAT IT HAD SCENTED US, BUT SHARIR EXPLAINED IT HAD ONLY PSYCHIC FACULTIES IMPLANTED BY KAL.

IT IS A MECHANICAL CREATURE SIMILAR TO AN ANDROID.

WHAT'S OUR DESTINATION?

WE WERE TO MEET AN AGENT FROM THE **MONASTERY OF LO** WHO WOULD TAKE US TO **THE CAPITAL OF SUKHSHAM PAD** TO MEET OTHER AGENTS WHO WOULD HELP FIND THE ZAPF OF JOHN SKALLY.

27

A LIGHT FOG BLEW IN FROM THE RIVER, SWIRLING AROUND US AS WE PASSED THE TALL ROCKS.
WE HEARD TINKLE OF A STRINGED INSTRUMENT PITCHED ABOVE THE ROARING WATERS AND A SOFT VOICE ROSE IN A SONG.
MY BELOVED, I WAITED SO LONG FOR YOU TO COME TO THIS LAND OF HAPPINESS.
SHARIR PUT OUT HIS HAND TO STOP ME.
IT'S LAOS, THE MATE OF THE TIGER.
SHE'S HARMLESS! LET ME GO TO HER!
DON'T LISTEN TO THE MAGICIAN OF LO. LET HIM GO TO HIS DOOM. STAY WITH ME FOREVER HERE IN PARADISE. YOU CAN ENJOY GREATER THINGS THAN YOU HAVE EVER KNOWN UPON YOUR PLANET EARTH!
I SAT DOWN PANTING. IT WAS IMPOSSIBLE FOR ANYONE TO RESIST HER HYPNOTIC EYES, EXCEPT SHARIR. THEY STOOD DEFYING EACH OTHER AND MY DESIRE FOR HER TORE ME AS I WATCHED AND FEARED FOR HER LIFE.
DON'T DESTROY HER!
29

SHE GAVE UP TO THE SUPERIOR POWER OF SHARIR THEN PROMISED TO TAKE US TO **KANWAL**.

IF YOU FALTER, I WILL NOT HESITATE TO DESTROY YOU!

MY DESIRE FOR HER *PASSED* AWAY, REPLACED BY CURIOSITY: WHY HAD THE MATE OF THE TIGER SUBMITTED SO READILY TO SHARIR?

MAYBE HE HAS TREMENDOUS POWERS AS HARRY GLAZER ONCE NOTED.

WE STOOD AT THE EDGE OF THE **RAGING RIVER**, WHICH WAS NOT REALLY WATER BUT TRILLIONS OF **TRAPPED SOULS**, STRUGGLING TO FIND THEIR WAY BACK TO LIFE.

THE RIVER IS A GREAT MAGNETIC FORCE. SHOULD WE TOUCH IT, WE INSTANTLY WILL BE SUCKED INTO THE STREAM AND WOULD STRUGGLE FOREVER TO BE RELEASED.

THIS RIVER IS A PRISON FOR SOULS, CREATED BY KAL TO TRAP THEM TO BE USED FOR LABOR WHEN NEEDED.

MANY WHO COME HERE ESCAPED THE TIGER BUT WERE TRAPPED IN THIS STREAM.

WE ROSE VERTICALLY HIGHER UNTIL WE WERE A MILE *ABOVE* THE ROARING RIVER. WE COULD FEEL THE SUCKING FORCE DRAGGING US DOWN. BUT SHARIR CAUGHT LAOS BY THE ARM AND WE LANDED SAFELY ON THE OTHER SIDE.

30

LAOS BECAME PALE BUT TURNED AND WENT DOWN THROUGH THE EXOTIC FOLIAGE.

THE BLUE SUNS CREATED VARIOUS PATTERNS IN THE SAND. AND SHARIR WARNED ME AGAINST PICKING THE ODOROUS FLOWERS.

I WAS PUZZLED. I THOUGHT THAT MATTER HAD A WAY OF PROTECTING ITSELF, BUT THE PROTECTION OF ENERGY WAS LESS DEFINED BECAUSE IT WAS ONLY A CONCEPT THAT BELONGS EVERYWHERE— EVEN WITHIN A MOVING SYSTEM SUCH AS ME.

THE UGLY INHABITANTS APPEARED IN ALL PLACES, AND THEIR GRUESOME APPEARANCE REPULSED ME.

THE HEAD OF THE VILLAGE ADVANCED TO MEET US. THE VILLAGERS KNEW LAOS TO BE THE **TIGER'S MATE**. BUT LAOS TOLD THEM WE WERE LOST AND LOOKING FOR MERCHANT FRIENDS. THE CHIEFTAIN LED US TO A LARGE DWELLING.

WE ENTERED THE HOUSE AND MET THE HOSTS, WHO WERE SURPRISED TO LEARN THAT LAOS WAS THE TIGER'S MATE. THEY DOUBTED HER LOYALTY BUT WERE ASSURED SHE WAS UNDER SHARIR'S CONTROL. THE HOSTS INFORMED US THAT JOHN SKALLY, THE **TUZA**, WAS BEING HELD AT THE **PRISON OF YEDO** — UNDER CONSTANT TORTURE.

WE'VE LEARNED THAT IF SKALLY DOES NOT GIVE UP HIS SECRET WITHIN FIVE PASSINGS OF THE TRIPLE SUNS, **KAL NIRANJAN** WILL COMPLETELY ANNIHILATE HIM.

FIVE DAYS?!

33

WE HAD TO GET THERE QUICKLY. I CLOSED MY EYES AND STARTED THINKING HARD ABOUT THE SCENE SHARIR WAS DESCRIBING.

THE PEACH-COLORED WHIRL OF DUSTS TURNED INTO A SPECTACLE OF MOVING OBJECTS LIKE A STREAM OF WATER THROUGH THE STREETS.

WE STOOD AT THE EDGE OF A BLUE-PINKISH LAKE.

THE GUARDS FLEW OVER THE CROWD OF BODIES OF MEN AND CREATURES OF DELUSION AND NIGHTMARE IN THE NEVER-ENDING SOUND OF WORSHIP OF THEIR **PHANTASMAGORIC GOD.**

SHARIR SHOWED US THE MYSTIC LAKE OF NIRANJAN WHICH GIVES POWER TO THOSE WHO BATHE IN IT, BUT FEW WERE GIVEN PERMISSION. THE TWO-HEADED GOD, ACCORDING TO SHARIR, LEAVES HIS THRONE DAILY TO GIVE A **DARSHAN** TO HIS PEOPLE.

THEY GATHER HERE IN BIG GROUPS TO RECEIVE HIS BLESSINGS.

34

SHARIR DROVE AWAY A **SUKHSHAMIAN DOG**. THEN WE HURRIEDLY WALKED BY THE LAKESIDE, BUT A GUARD, WHO GLIDED OVER US, SENT US INTO HIDING UNDER THE TREES.

HOW MUCH FURTHER?

WE'RE ALMOST THERE. PERHAPS FIVE OR MAYBE TEN MINUTES.

APPARENTLY, OUR PRESENCE WAS KNOWN. WE MADE OUR WAY THROUGH THE UNDERBRUSH. BUT UPON REACHING THE EDGE OF THE LAKE, **VISRNA** CREPT OUT TO SIGNAL THE BOAT ON THE OTHER SIDE OF THE LAKE.

A SAILING VESSEL MOVED TOWARD US UNTIL IT WAS NEAR ENOUGH, AND A YELLOWISH MAN WAVED US ABOARD. WE RODE ACROSS THE LAKE TO THE OTHER SIDE.

WE PULLED INTO A DOCK UNDER A BLUFF AND PUSHED OUR WAY BETWEEN ROCKS, FINALLY COMING OUT ABOVE A PATH SURROUNDED BY PUPLE VEGETATION.

WE WENT UP TO THE DOOR. VISRNA NODDED TWICE AND THE DOOR OPENED. DHIRADA'S FACE IS BOTH HAPPY AND SAD.

WE MEET AT LAST SHARIR OF LO. YOU ARRIVED JUST IN TIME, FOR THE **TIME MAKERS** ARE SEARCHING FOR YOU. THEY DON'T KNOW YOU YET BUT ARE AWARE YOU ARE AN ENEMY.

THANK YOU DHIRADA OF SUKHSHAM. WE NEED TO REST AND HIDE FOR SEVERAL HOURS UNTIL READY TO RESCUE JOHN SKALLY AND RECOVER THE SECRET DIARY.

THAT IS THE HOME OF **DHIRADA**, A REBEL LEADER HERE IN SUKHSHAM. HE HAS WORKED SECRETLY WITH THE MAGICIANS OF LO FOR YEARS. DO YOU KNOW HIM, SIRE?

ONLY BY NAME. IS HE TRUSTWORTHY ENOUGH TO HIDE US FOR SEVERAL HOURS?

WE WILL WORK TOGETHER AND I THINK I CAN HELP YOU IN MY SMALL WAY. I LIVE ALONE HERE BUT HAVE FRIENDS EVERY WHERE. TO BE ALONE IS GOOD FOR THE MIND.

YOU HAVE AN INTUITIVE MIND, MY GOOD FRIEND. AN INTUITIVE MIND IN ITS CREATIVITY NEEDS TO BE IN SECLUSION, NOT SOCIETY NOR THE WORLD OF KAL NIRANJAN.

35

THE MOB MIND IS BOTH CRUDE AND UN-DISCIPLINED. THE GROUP MIND COULD NOT BE RATIONAL OR CREATIVE. REASON AND CREATIVITY AT THEIR BEST ARE FUNCTIONS OF THE INDIVIDUAL MIND IN ISOLATION.

YOU ARE RIGHT, SHARIR. ONLY THOSE WHO HAVE SUFFERED BUT SUCCEEDED IN CREATING IDEAS KNOW THE BENEFIT OF ISOLATION, FOR LIFE IS IN LOVE ONLY WITH ITSELF.

THE MAGICIAN DOESN'T RELY ON EXPERIENCE. HE ONLY FAVORS GOD OR SOUL. THE TIME MAKERS ARE ONLY OBSESSED WITH LEARNING AND BEING SUCCESSFUL. THE MAGICIAN STRONGLY SEEKS TO FIND BALANCE WITH NATURE AND PEACE IN IT.

HE IS NOT WILLING TO LEARN FROM EXPERIENCE, FOR THE UNIVERSE HAS NOTHING TO TEACH HIM. HE ACCEPTS THINGS AS THEY COME AND KNOWS IN ADVANCE WHAT TO DO WITH THEM IN ACCORDANCE WITH HIS BELIEF.

WELL SAID. WHAT DO YOU WANT FROM ME?

CALL A MEETING FOR ALL THE MAGICIANS IN SUKHSHAM WHO SYMPATHIZE WITH YOU IN YOUR FIGHT FOR FREEDOM.

I CAN DO THAT BUT THERE ARE ONLY A HANDFUL OF US NOW. KAL NIRANJAN HAS ELIMINATED MOST OF US.

GUARDS FLEW OVER THE ROOFTOP BUT DIS-
APPEARED INTO THE HORIZON. THE FOG
PUT UP BY SHARIR SERVED AS RADAR
SCREEN AND CAMOUFLAGE AGAINST INTRU-
DERS.

SHARIR MENTIONED A VIEW SCREEN BEHIND THE WALL AND
DHIRADA LAUGHED SOFTLY AND SLAPPED HIS LEGS.

YOU ARE INDEED A GREAT MAGICIAN,
SHARIR. I'M GLAD WE'RE FRIENDS
AND NOT FOES. I'LL OPEN IT
AND WE'LL WATCH OUR ENEMIES
TOGETHER!

THE VIEW SCREEN FLICKERED WITH LIGHTS WHICH TURNED OUT TO BE A GROUP OF MAGICIANS LED
BY TABA. SHARIR DISCUSSED THE PLAN OF RESCUE TO THEM, AND ON THE SCREEN WE ALSO SAW
THE KAL INTERROGATING JOHN SKALLY WHO REFUSED TO DISCLOSE THE SECRET OF THE DIARY.

SHARIR STUDIED THE NEW DATUM
AND TOLD EACH MAGICIAN WHAT TO
DO. THEY LEFT THROUGH THE SCREEN,
FOLLOWED BY VISRNA AND EZAN.

WE PROJECTED OURSELVES THROUGH THE VIEW SCREEN,
OUT INTO THE DARK SUKHSHAMIAN NIGHT.
SHARIR CIRCLED THE CITY AND LAOS POINTED A DIREC-
TION AND DESCENDED THROUGH ATMOSPHERE.

THE ONLY FEAR THAT SHARIR HAD WAS OF THE **TALONS OF TIME** AND THEIR MACHINES. THEY COULD THICKEN THE ATMOSPHERE AND CONTROL THE WHOLE UNIVERSE. WE THEN BEGAN OUR WAY THROUGH THE TUNNEL, WITH LAOS LEADING.

WE PASSED THE GATES INTO THE FORBIDDEN **FIELD OF YEDIO**, BUT THE OPENING WHERE IT USED TO BE SEEMED TO BE SEALED. I RELUCTANTLY SAT AND WATCHED SHARIR OPEN THE SEALED WALL WITH HIS MAGIC.

THE SIDE OF THE WALL MELTED AND GAVE WAY TO A BLACK OPENING. WE CRAWLED THROUGH THIS LONG TUNNEL OF DRIPPING BLACK LAVA.

REACHING A BLANK WALL, LAOS STOOD IN A PUDDLE OF COLD WATER.

THIS IS THE END OF THE TUNNEL.

THIS WILL LEAD US INTO THE DUNGEON WHERE JOHN SKALLY IS IMPRISONED.

39

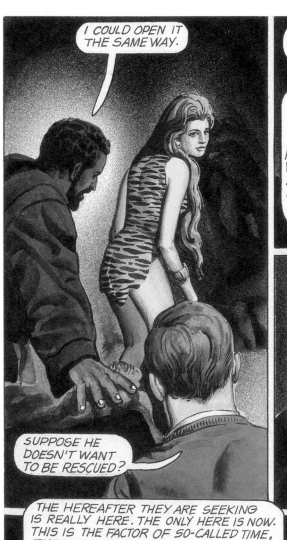

I COULD OPEN IT THE SAME WAY.

SUPPOSE HE DOESN'T WANT TO BE RESCUED?

THE WILL TO SURVIVE IS VERY STRONG IN ALL SOULS.

I KNOW JOHN SKALLY TO BE STRONGER THAN MOST, AND HE COULD SURVIVE THE CRUDEST OF PUNISHMENT MOST PEOPLE ARE AFRAID OF.

THE DESIRE TO ESCAPE FROM THE REMEMBERED SELF IS SO DEEP-SEATED IN MOST PEOPLE THAT EVEN IF THEY DO, THEY ARE SURPRISED THAT THERE IS NO LOSS OF EXPERIENCE FROM THEIR KNOWN WORLD. THE ESCAPE IS FOR NOTHING.

THE HEREAFTER THEY ARE SEEKING IS REALLY HERE. THE ONLY HERE IS NOW. THIS IS THE FACTOR OF SO-CALLED TIME, THE NOW-FIELD WHICH EXTENDS OUTWARD INTO SPACE THROUGH ENERGY YOU PROJECT FROM YOUR MIND.

BUT THE FIELD OF THE HERE DOES NOT EXTEND THUS, IT REMAINS AS LATENT ENERGY CARRIED WITHIN YOU ALWAYS.

THIS HOWEVER, MUST BE DISCOVERED FROM YOUR OWN PERSONAL INDIVIDUAL EXPERIENCE.

40

ROUGH HANDS PULLED LAOS FROM MY ARMS. I WAS TERRIFIED. LAOS AND I WATCHED THE FANTASTIC GUARDS EXAMINING THE WALLS, BUT WE HELD OUR THOUGHTS SO AS NOT TO DISCLOSE THE TUNNEL. THEY GAVE UP AND HUSTLED US OUT OF THE DOOR OF THE CELL AND BROUGHT US IN FRONT OF A *TIME MAKER*. I WANTED TO CHOKE HIM BUT HE READ MY THOUGHTS.

I READ YOUR THOUGHTS EARTHLING. THERE'S NOTHING YOU CAN DO NOW.

EKAL, THE CHIEF OF *SUKH-SHAMIAN POLICE*, HAD THE POWER TO DECIDE, WOULD FEED LAOS TO THE *VULTURES OF YADL*. BUT THE JUDGEMENT WOULD BE MADE BY KAL, AND A HOLIDAY WOULD BE DECLARED TO CELEBRATE THEIR VICTORY OVER OUR CAPTURE. I WAS IRKED.

EKAL TOLERATED MY CONDUCT AND ALLOWED ME TO TALK.

THERE'S NOTHING THAT YOU COULD DO NOW, *EKAL*. WE OF EARTH ARE IMMORTAL TUZAS DWELLING IN THE IDEAL OF *HAPPY NOW*. WE ARE *BEINGS*, BUT YOU ARE *EXISTENTS* LIVING IN THE REGRESSION OF LIFE... THE STILLNESS OF MOTION.

YOU WILL NEVER CAPTURE SHARIR. HE ALREADY ES- CAPED AND IS NOW ON HIS WAY TO EARTH!

OUR WORLD WILL CONTINUE WITHIN THE DURATION OF TIME WHILE YOUR WORLD WILL PASS AWAY. THEREFORE, IT DOESN'T MATTER HOW MANY LIKE MYSELF YOU DESTROY, FOR THE *RACE OF MAN* WILL *NEVER BE DESTROYED*.

42

EKAL BECAME FURIOUS. INSTANTLY, HIS GUARDS WHISKED US TO A FLOATING ELEVATOR THAT LIFTED US WITH GREAT SPEED INSIDE THE ROUND TURRET OF A TOWER OVERLOOKING THE PRISON OF YEDIO.

LAOS AND I LAY EXHAUSTED ON THE FLOOR, KISSING AND EMBRACING EACH OTHER TO FIND COMFORT.

LAOS SLEPT. I EXAMINED THE WINDOW AND SAW THROUGH IT THE GUARDS CONSTANTLY ON WATCH.

STRANGE THINGS WERE WOVEN INTO MY MIND.

CARS WITH INVISIBLE MOTORS, A BRIDGE THAT DISAPPEARED INTO THE WATER... ALL KEPT ME WONDERING.

THERE WAS NO MEASUREMENT OF TIME HERE COMPARED TO EARTH. THERE WAS ONLY VAST CHANGING SEQUENCES OF EVENTS THAT COULD NOT REPRESENT IN REAL TIME OR CHANGING SEQUENCES, THE CHANGE OF STATE FROM A FUTURE TO A PAST CONDITION.

43

I STARED ACROSS THE MULTI-COLORED LANDSCAPE AND THOUGHT HARD. THESE CHANGES ARE NOT REAL REPRESENTATIONS OF ABSTRACT TIME BUT ONLY LISTS OF PAST HAPPENINGS IN PEOPLE'S LIVES. THEY ARE DURATION MEASURED BY MOVEMENTS IN SPACE.

MAN THEREFORE ONLY LIMITS HIS MOVEMENT IN TIME. THE MAN THAT OBSERVES DATA FILLS ALL PARTS OF SPACE EXTENDED IN TIME. ONE SHOULD PASS RELATIVITY AND ACT ALONE, AS I, PRISONER, WITHOUT OBSERVERS BEING CALLED IN TO ASSIST.

THIS WORLD IS TIMELESS. ENERGIES PASSING FROM SPIRIT TO BODY SHOULD NOT EXIST, BECAUSE TO OBSERVE THEM AS SUCH ONLY RESTRICTS. THE IGNORANT, WHO DOESN'T KNOW THIS, WOULD BELIEVE THEM REALITY.

YOUR RANGE OF ATTENTION IS LIMITED ONLY BY THE LIMIT OF YOUR FIELD OF OBSERVATION!

LIGHTS, COLOR, PAIN, TASTES, SMELLS, AND SOUNDS ARE ONLY SENSE DATUM RESTRICTED IN TIME AND SPACE. MY THOUGHTS WERE INTERRUPTED. I FROZE AS THE LANDSCAPE SUDDENLY CHANGED. IT WASN'T THERE ANYMORE EXCEPT FOR A BLACK CLOUD AND A GOLDEN MIST. FROM OUT OF THE FOG...

THAT WAS SHARIR'S VOICE. I LOOKED AROUND THE TOWER BUT COULD NOT SEE HIM. I CLAWED AT THE GLASS.

SHARIR! WHERE ARE YOU? WHERE ARE YOU?

44

MY SHOUTS ECHOED INSIDE THE TOWER AND LAOS PACIFIED ME. I CRIED OUT THAT SUKHSHAM WAS ONLY AN ILLUSION. SHE ROSE TO VIEW THE LANDSCAPE BUT MUMBLED...

BELOVED, I SEE NOTHING BUT GUARDS FLYING AROUND THE TOWER AND THE CITY. DID YOU SEE A VISION?

SHE WAS RIGHT. THERE WAS NOTHING BUT THE CRAZY COLOR OF THE MOUNTAIN AND THRONGS OF PEOPLE IN THEIR FRENZIED MOVEMENTS.

I THOUGHT THAT THE SECRET OF TIME HAD BEEN REVEALED TO ME. I LOOKED AT LAOS AND WONDERED IF SHE COULD STILL BE TRUSTED, BUT THAT DIDN'T MATTER FOR MY MIND WAS NOW COMPLETELY BLANKED.

PERHAPS I'M GOING STIR-CRAZY BY BEING IN A ROUND CELL.

I FELT AS THOUGH I WAS STANDING ON THE EDGE OF THE WORLD, LOOKING OUT OVER A DEEP GULCH.

I LOLLED ON LAOS'S LAP. HER HAND STROKING MY HEAD COMFORTED ME.

♪ THEN SLEEP MY LOVE. AFTERWARDS YOU WILL BE REFRESHED AND ALL WILL COME BACK TO YOUR MIND. LA LA LA LA ♪♪

INSTANTLY, I FELL INTO A DEEP SLUMBER, DREAMING I WAS STANDING ALONE AT THE VERY EDGE OF TIME WHICH SHOOK ME AND TERRIFIED ME.

THE STRONG FEAR MADE ME FEEL HELPLESS, PUSHING ME INTO AN ENDLESS LAKE AGAINST MY WILL. I WAS CAUGHT IN A MOTIONLESS CENTER WHERE PAST AND FUTURE COULD NOT BE RECOGNIZED.

ALL MY EXPERIENCES ON EARTH PUT ME DEEPER INTO A TRAP WITHIN TIME. I COULD NOT TELL WHETHER I WAS USING MY UNREALIZED POWERS AS SOUL TO CREATE A SELF-HYPNOTIC ILLUSION, BELIEVED TO BE LIGHT ITSELF.

I PASSED THE THINKING STAGE AGAIN AND WAS IN THE BLANKNESS OF SPACE WITHIN A SHINY GOLDEN WEB.

I STRUGGLED TO BE FREED FROM IT, BUT IT CHANGED INTO WAVES OF LIGHT LIKE A MOTION PICTURE SCREEN WITHOUT ANY SCENE. THESE MILLIONS OF TINY GLEAMING LIGHTS WERE REFLECTIONS OF SOMETHING ELSE.

SHARIR, SURROUNDED BY DHIRADA AND VISRNA, APPEARED ON THE SCREEN, WORKING OVER A GRAYISH FIGURE WHICH COULD BE JOHN SKALLY. IT WAS LIKE A WORLD WITHIN MY MIND.

THESE WAVE PICTURES OF THINGS I ALREADY KNEW WERE PROVIDED BY SOMETHING WHICH EXISTED APART FROM ME. THE PANORAMA SWITCHED AGAIN, AND I WAS WALKING DOWN THE HIGHWAY OF KANWAL, ESCORTED BY WARRIOR-PRIESTS.

THE ROAD WAS CRAMMED WITH HORDES OF PILGRIMS WHO CAME TO KANWAL THROUGH MILLIONS OF MILES OF SPACE TO SEEK THE BLESSINGS OF **KAL NIRANJAN**—THEIR GOD.

FIRST CAME THE FANFARE, FOLLOWED BY THE TWO-HEADED GOD SEATED ON A **SHOULDER-CARRIED CHAIR.**

MAKE WAY! MAKE WAY! THE GREAT KAL APPROACHES!

THE EVIL EYES OF KAL SEARCHED THE MULTITUDE OF FACES AND STOPPED ON ME.

47

I WOKE UP WITHOUT REMEMBERING ANYTHING EXCEPT THE KAL LOOKING AT ME.

LAOS CRIED AND CARESSED ME SOFTLY WITH HER HANDS.

SHE KEPT MY THOUGHTS FOCUSED ON HER, BUT THE HORROR OF SUKHSHAM WOULD NOT LEAVE ME. I WAS AWARE THAT SOMETHING NEAR WAS WATCHING ME WITH SATISFACTION. I FOUGHT THIS SELF-INDULGENCE AROUSING ME BUT WAS HELPLESS AGAINST MY GREAT DESIRE FOR LAOS.

THOUGHTS STARTED FLOWING. I KNEW THAT BY **PROJECTION** WE COULD ESCAPE, BUT THE FEELING OF SUSPENSION OVERWHELMED ME. LAOS BECAME SAD AND SURPRISED.

I HAVE AN IDEA. WE COULD ESCAPE THIS TOWER AND SUKHSHAM!

LAOS DID NOT LIKE MY IDEA, BUT I REMINDED HER HOW SHARIR'S MAGIC SAVED US FROM THE HOSTILE DWARFS IN THE VILLAGE OF TRETA. LAOS DOUBTED AND THIS MADE ME ANGRY.

WE FACE DESTRUCTION AND ALL YOU WANT TO DO IS MAKE LOVE?

PLEASE, DON'T BE ANGRY WITH ME. I'LL DO WHATEVER YOU SAY, BUT I REALLY DON'T KNOW HOW YOU DO IT.

48

I TOLD HER SHE WOULD BE GIVEN A THICK BODY AND A CLOTHING TO PROTECT IT FROM THE CHANGING WEATHER. SHE LISTENED WITH AMAZEMENT.

LAOS LOOKED STEADILY AT ME AS I DESCRIBED THE SOCIETIES OF EARTH PEOPLE, THEIR BEHAVIOR, AND HOW THEY TRAVEL AROUND THE COUNTRY. SHE BECAME SATISFIED AND WE BEGAN CONCENTRATING.

THERE WAS A SLIGHT MOVEMENT OF OUR LIGHT BODIES AND I TRIED TO BRING MY THOUGHTS TOGETHER TO PROJECT US TO EARTH. THEN ANOTHER MOVEMENT FOLLOWED, AS IF A RUG HAD LIFTED US INTO SPACE, WHILE I WAS HOLDING A SCENE OF TALKING WITH HARRY GLAZER.

THE SWIFT MOTION STOPPED ABRUPTLY. UPON OPENING MY EYES, I WAS SURPRISED TO SEE MYSELF SURROUNDED BY GRAY FOG.

GROTESQUE SHADOWS HORRIFIED ME, AS IF WAITING TO SEIZE ME, BUT I SUBDUED THEM. I FELT HELPLESS AND WISHED TO BE SUCCESFUL AS SHARIR IN PROJECTION.

49

SUCH EMPTINESS FILLED ME THAT EVEN MY MIND REFUSED TO FUNCT- ION. MY LONELINESS BECAME OVERWHELMING.

I HAD LOST HER, PROBABLY IN THE PRESSURES AND CURRENTS OF SUKHSHAM. I COULD NOT THINK THAT SHE HAD BETRAYED ME. I JUST DIDN'T KNOW WHAT HAD GONE WRONG.

LAOS! WHERE ARE YOU? COME TO ME!

THE STILLNESS OF THE FOG WAS TERRIFYING AND SIFTED IN- TO MY BODY AS IF TO KILL IT. I FELT I HAD REACHED THE END OF MY LIFE. THEN I HEARD WHIS- PERINGS IN THE DISTANT MIST AND UNIDENTIFIED SHADOWS CREPT AWAY IN THE FOG, RUSTLING.

I HOPED THAT IT WAS LAOS BUT IT WAS NOT HER. CONSCIOUSNESS, SENSATION, PASSION, EFFORTS, AND OTHERS ARE PRO- DUCED IN THIS FANTASTIC WORLD AND I EXPERIENCED THEM AS TRUTH, FOR THEY ARE THE LOW AND THE HIGH PITCHES OF MY CONSCIOUS- NESS.

50

I BECAME AWARE OF DURATION, AND STEP BY STEP I WAS LED TO UNDERSTAND TIME AND SELF. TIME INVOLVES MOVEMENT. AND AT THAT MOMENT, I WAS FROZEN IN THE REALM OF TIME. I COULD NOT THINK ABOUT TIME WITHOUT THINKING OF MOVEMENT. TIME WAS CONCEIVED AS BEING COMPOSED OF PAST, PRESENT, AND FUTURE. FUTURE MOVES TO THE PRESENT AND BECOMES THE PRESENT. THEN IT MOVES INTO THE PAST. THESE INDICATED CONSTANT CHANGE, PROGRESSION, SUCCESSION, AND MOVEMENT.

BUT I DIDN'T KNOW WHERE I WAS. THIS COULD BE THE PRISON WHERE KAL HAD THROWN ME WHEN I HAD ESCAPED FROM THE TOWER.

I REALIZED THAT THIS WAS THE PRISON OF DARKNESS, AND THE RUSTLING SOUNDS WERE THE SUKHSHAM DOGS GUARDING ME TO SEE THAT I DIDN'T ESCAPE THIS PLACE. BUT HOW I HAD ESCAPED FROM THE TOWER HAD PUZZLED ME. KAL NIRANJAN HAD IMPRISONED ME WITH THE ELEMENT OF TIME.

IT WAS THE SAME AS BEING PLUNGED INTO A DUNGEON, AS JOHN SKALLY HAD BEEN OR PROMETHEUS FOR STEALING THE FIRES OF HEAVEN FOR THE SONS OF MAN.

IF THIS WERE TRUE THEN I WAS IN ETERNITY, AND TIME AND MOVEMENT WERE NOT IDENTICAL.

MY MISTAKE WAS IN TRYING TO PROJECT LAOS WHO WAS AN ANDROID NOT CAPABLE OF CONCENTRATING. I DIDN'T KNOW WHY SHE HAD DISAPPEARED.

SLOWLY MY THOUGHTS CAME BACK TO TIME AGAIN. I SURMISED THAT IN ALL MOVEMENTS, THERE WAS SUCCESSION OF BEFORE AND AFTER MOVEMENT...

THE UNIFORM PASSAGE OF MOTION WITH ITS PAST AND FUTURE MADE UP WHAT WE CALL TIME IN ALL THE UNIVERSES, INCLUDING SUKHSHAM.

IF I TOOK OUT MOVEMENT FROM VARIOUS CHANGES AND THOUGHT OF NOTHING BUT ABSTRACT MOVEMENT ITSELF, I WOULD HAVE REALITY IN ABSOLUTE TIME.

IF I HAD A PERFECT UNDERSTANDING OF THESE LAWS, IT WOULD BE POSSIBLE TO CALCULATE AND TO FORESEE WHAT WOULD HAPPEN TO EACH OF THESE IMAGES. THE FUTURE OF IMAGES MUST BE CONTAINED IN THE PRESENT.

THE SUKHSHAM DOGS BECAME RESTLESS AROUND ME, AND BEYOND THEM WAS LAUGHTER LIKE THE FAINT SOUND OF WIND. I KNEW IT WAS KAL NIRANJAN. HIS LAUGHTER — OR SOMETHING THAT WAS IN OR BEHIND THE LAUGHTER.

THE SOUND SWELLED AND FILLED ME AND THROBBED IN THE CHANNELS OF MY **NURI SARUP**. IT ALSO FILLED THE FOG WHERE I STOOD AND SEEMED TO BE COMING FROM DEEP WITHIN ME.

SUDDENLY I REMEMBERED SOMETHING. THE BEFORE AND AFTER STATES OF PHYSICAL, PHYSIOLOGICAL, PSYCHOLOGICAL STATES ARE REVEALED IN THE CONCEPT OF TIME. THIS WAS WHY I COULD NOTICE THE PASSAGE OF TIME WHEN IN THE MOTIONLESS STATE, SURROUNDED BY A MOTIONLESS WORLD, BUT CONCENTRATED ON THE PRESENCE AND SUCCESSION OF MY INTERNAL THOUGHTS AND EMOTIONS.

THIS COULD MEAN I COULD ESCAPE THIS TRAP IF MY MIND CONCENTRATED ON SOMETHING BETTER, THEN I THOUGHT OF LAOS.

SHE WAS LOST BUT WE COULD BE TOGETHER AGAIN.

I CONCENTRATED HARD ON BEING BESIDE LAOS, HOLDING THIS IMAGE STILL AND PUTTING MYSELF INTO IT. I REALIZED THAT **INTELLECTUALIZED TIME IS SPACE**, AND INTELLIGENCE WORKS ONLY UPON THE FANTASY OF DURATION, NOT DURATION ITSELF.

53

I KNEW THAT TO PASS FROM INTELLECTION TO VISION, OR FROM RELATIVE TO ABSOLUTE WAS NOT GETTING OUTSIDE OF TIME BUT GETTING INTO DURATION OR ETERNITY.

THE ESSENCE OF TIME IS MOVEMENT, AND I HAD TO EXIST IN IT WHEREVER IN THIS UNIVERSE I WAS DURING THAT PARTICULAR MOMENT. SUDDENLY...

THE GARDEN OF THE TEMPLE!

TWELVE WOMEN IN PROCESSION WALKED TO THE ALTAR AND HALTED WHILE THE GOLDEN-HAIRED MAID STOOPED TO PLACE A LAMP AT THE FEET OF THE STATUE OF KAL.

THE WOMAN SPRINKLED THE LIGHTED LAMP AND THE FIRE FLARED INTO A MULTI-COLORED FLAME. BLUISH GNOMES BURST OUT OF FLAME AND DANCED ABOUT THE STATUE.

54

THE MELODY STIRRED ME. THE WOMEN WERE SWAYING THEIR BODIES AND MOANING IN ECSTASY. THE GOLDEN BLONDE STOOD UP AND REMOVED HER ROBE.

HER BODY GLEAMED AND I WAS ALARMED, FOR THE GOLDEN IVORY FIGURE WAS FAMILIAR. SHE DANCED LIKE THE GENTLE FLOWING OF WATER AND HER BODY WAS A TWISTING RHYTHM OF BEAUTY. BUT WHEN SHE TURNED HER FACE, I JUMPED TO MY FEET TO PURSUE HER.

LAOS LAOS

THE SCENE SUDDENLY VANISHED.

WEAKENED, I FELL PROSTRATED BEFORE THE STATUE. A LOW AND HIDEOUS LAUGHTER GREW WILDER AND IT RACKED THE TEMPLE.

BWA HA HA HA HA HA HA

KAL, BRING HER BACK TO ME!

THE LAUGHTER CEASED ABRUPTLY.

YOU MORTAL FOOL. DID YOU THINK YOU COULD BEAT THE GREAT KAL? DID YOU BELIEVE THAT SHARIR, THE UGLY MAGICIAN, WAS A GREATER MAGICIAN THAN I?

55

KAL MOCKED THE MAGICIANS BUT GLO-RIFIED HIMSELF. HE DESPISED SHA-RIR AND OTHERS WHO TRIED TO UNLOCK THE SECRET OF TIME, AND STATED THAT HE AND THE TIME MAKERS ONLY KNEW THE SECRET.

THE ESSENCE OF A THING IS KNOWN BY ITS PRO-PERTIES. THE MEASURE MUST CORRESPOND IN KIND TO THE THING MEASURED.

WE, THE TIME MAKERS OBTAINED THE KNOWLEDGE OF TIME BY OB-SERVING THE MOVEMENTS OF THE MATERIAL WORLD AND SUCCESSION OF CHANGES THERE.

WHEN CONSCIOUS OF MOVEMENT, YOU ARE AWARE OF THE PASSAGE OF TIME, WHEN NOT CONSCIOUS OF IT, YOU ARE UNCONS-CIOUS OF ITS PASSAGE.

YOU USE STANDARDS TO MEASURE TIME BY THE MOVEMENT OF YOUR PLANETARY SYSTEM, STARS, TIDES, CLOCKS AND SUN.

WHEN VIEWED AS AN EFFECT OF POSSIBLE MOVEMENT, THIS TIME IS FALSE TIME. TRUE TIME IS THE ABSTRACT CAUSE OF ACTUAL MOVEMENT OF PAST, PRESENT, AND FUTURE OCCURING IN THE EXISTING WORLD.

56

LAOS HAD NEVER LEFT THE TOWER BECAUSE SHE HAD FAILED TO PROJECT HERSELF. THE GUARDS TOOK HER TO THE PRISON CHIEF, EKAL, WHO BROUGHT HER TO THE TEMPLE TO DANCE.

THEY GAVE ME COMPLETE FREEDOM AND I CAME TO THIS HOME OF MY FRIEND MARTIS.

MARTIS CAME IN AND INVITED ME TO STAY IN HIS HOME.

I THANKED HIM FOR HIS HOSPITALITY AND PROMISED TO STAY WITH LAOS UNTIL WE WERE READY TO LEAVE.

LAOS AND I ENJOYED THE GREENISH MOON IN THE GARDEN OF THIS WORLD WHERE IMAGES BECOME REAL ONLY IF I BECOME CONSCIOUS OF THEM.

IF THIS WERE TRUE, EVEN THE **LIGHT BODY** WAS ONLY AN IMAGE LIKE MY PHYSICAL BODY. SO IF I ELIMINATED THIS **NURI SARUP**, THE WORLD OF SUKHSHAM WOULD VANISH.

IT WAS POSSIBLE TO CHANGE THE SURROUNDING IMAGES. THESE EXTERNAL IMAGES ALSO INFLUENCED THE IMAGE OF NURI SARUP AS IT INFLUENCED THEM, GIVING BACK MOVEMENT TO THEM.

AS A CENTER OF ACTION, THE LIGHT BODY COULD MOVE OTHER OBJECTS—AND COULD EVEN DESTROY THEM.

BUT IT COULD NOT GIVE BIRTH TO IMAGES ALREADY CREATED BY OTHERS.

LAOS'S PLANS FOR OUR FUTURE IN SUKHSHAM WERE IMAGES CONNECTED TO TIME.

I DIDN'T GIVE MUCH THOUGHT TO THEM.

TIME MOVES FORWARD IN A PROGRESSIVE SUCCESSION, WITHOUT PARTS THAT SIMULTANEOUSLY MOVE WITHIN IT.

IMAGES THEREFORE MUST WORK WITHIN ITS FRAMEWORK. THE PARTS OF TIME SUCCEED EACH OTHER IN A BEFORE and AFTER FASHION AS FUTURE, PRESENT, AND PAST.'

HENCE, THERE IS NO BEFORE OR AFTER IN THE PRESENT, WHICH IS THE POINT OF TERMINATION FOR THE PAST AND FUTURE.

SINCE NO TWO PARTS COULD EXIST IN THE FUTURE AND PAST, THEY COULD NOT DUPLICATE THEMSELVES IN THE IMMEDIATE PRESENT.

I SPOKE LOUDLY BUT LAOS WAS NOT LISTENING. SHE TALKED ABOUT BUILDING A NEW HOME, BUT I DIDN'T CARE ABOUT THIS AND SHE SCOLDED ME. SHE SENSED I WAS UNHAPPY.

I WILL GO WITH YOU IF YOU ARE NOT HAPPY HERE.

I FEARED FOR SHARIR, LAOS, AND MYSELF, BUT LAOS LAUDED ME FOR MY ACCOMPLISHMENT IN PROJECTION AND NOTED THAT KAL WANTED ME BY HIS SIDE ONLY TO DEFEAT SHARIR AND THE MAGICIANS.

60

GAOS'S WOMANLY INSTINCT THWARTED MY IDEALS, AND I NOW BECAME SUBMISSIVE TO HER DESIRE.

WE COULD STAY HERE FOREVER IN THIS PARADISE.

WE CAN HUNT, FIGHT, AND LIVE TOGETHER!

BUT THE PROBLEM OF TIME AGAIN ENTERED MY THOUGHTS, AND I CONTINUED EXPLAINING.

IN ORDER TO EXIST IN TIME, ONE SHOULD IGNORE IT. ONE IS TRAPPED IN IT BY BEING A PART OF IT.

MOVEMENTS DO NOT EXIST BY THEMSELVES. THERE IS MOVEMENT BECAUSE SOMETHING SUCH AS BODIES MOVE.

ALL BODIES IN NATURE, PHYSICAL OR LIGHT BODIES, EXIST IN TIME BECAUSE THEY ARE THE BEARERS OF MOTION. AND CHANGE IN THE UNIVERSE IS A GATHERING OF ALL BODIES SO IT COULD PROPERLY EXIST IN TIME. TIME IS THEN SUITABLE TO THE UNIVERSE AND TO ALL BEINGS WHICH ARE PART OF THE UNIVERSE.

THE SOUL CAN NOT BE AFFECTED BY TIME AND CAN LIVE IN AND OUT OF IT.

IT IS THE ONLY TRUE SUBSTANCE WHICH IS UNTOUCHED BY **MATTER, ENERGY, TIME,** AND **SPACE.** BUT IT CAN MAKE, COLLECT, AND PROJECT IMAGES.

WHAT ARE YOU TRYING TO PROVE, PEDDAR ZASKQ?

TO FIND THE KEY TO UNLOCK TIME AND BE ABLE TO SLIDE BACK TO EARTH AGAIN.

61

THE STRANGER, THOUGH A FREQUENT VISITOR IN THE PAST, HAD FORGOTTEN THE STREETS IN THIS TOWN.

HIS EYES BORE INTO ME AS HE TOLD ME I WAS IN GREAT CONFLICT: TO LIVE WITH LAOS OR BETRAY MY FRIENDS. IT WAS MY DECISION, BUT HE REMINDED ME TO GET THE KEY WHICH CONTROLS TIME. IMAGES HAD MUCH TO DO WITH THIS KEY.

SLIGHT CHANGES IN A CERTAIN IMAGE – YOURSELF – ALTER YOUR PERCEPTION OF THE UNIVERSE. THIS IMAGE OCCUPIES THE CENTER OF YOU. AND AT EACH MOVEMENT, EVERYTHING CHANGES AS THOUGH BY A TURN OF KALEIDOSCOPE.

IN THIS UNIVERSE, HOWEVER, ARE THE SAME IMAGES. EACH ONE REFERS TO ITSELF. THEY INFLUENCE EACH OTHER, BUT THE EFFECT IS ALWAYS IN PRORORTION TO THE CAUSE, THE MAN SAID.

THE DIFFERENCE BETWEEN THE **IDEAL** AND THE **REAL** IS CAUSED BY ENDLESSLY CHANGING PERCEPTION.

THIS IS EXTERNAL REALITY!

YOU CAN NOT SEPARATE THE INTERIOR FROM THE EXTERIOR, BECAUSE THEY BELONG TO ONE SET AND DOING SO WILL ONLY CREATE HAVOC WITHIN THE INDIVIDUAL.

TIME IS NATURALLY REAL BUT A FALSE IMAGE, BELONGING TO THE EXTERNAL REALITY. WHAT YOU SEE AS THE WORLD IMAGE IS YOUR WAY OF INTERPRETING IT – A PRODUCT OF YOUR EXTERNAL SENSES – AN ILLUSION.

PROBLEMS BORN OF IT CAN NOT BE SOLVED, **BUT** PROBLEMS MADE WITHIN IT COULD BE DISSOLVED.

TIME AND SPACE ARE ABSTRACTION. AND WHEN ABSTRACTION IS CONSIDERED REAL, IT CONTRADICTS ITSELF.

THE PSYCHIC APPARATUS OF MAN IMPOSES THE CONDITION OF TIME IN OUR PERCEPTION ABOUT THE WORLD, OTHERWISE WE COULD NOT PERCEIVE IT.

BUILDING AND SERVING THE FUTURE ARE ONLY SYMBOLS OF ONE'S ATTITUDE OF HIS OWN PRESENT.

63

THE STRANGER WHO CALLED HIMSELF THE **WANDERING MAGI** WARNED ME NOT TO ALLOW **KAL** TO USE ME TO CAPTURE THE MAGICIANS.

HE GAVE ME THE KEY TO THE SECRET OF TIME BUT I WASN'T LISTENING.

FINDING THE SECRET WOULD SAVE ME FROM TOTAL DESTRUCTION.

THEN HE DISAPPEARED INTO THE CROWD. FOR A WHILE I STOOD WATCHING THEN LEAPED FORWARD TO FOLLOW HIM. IT WAS **SHARIR**, WHO DISAPPEARED AMONG THE SCREAMING CROWD THAT PUSHED ME TOWARD THE SHRINE TO PRAY.

THE ONLY REALITY WAS THE LIVING TUZA.

I FOUND THIS BY ABSTRACTING THE TWO OPPOSITE DIRECTIONS, WHICH BECOME PATHS, IT DEPENDED ONLY UPON THE TUZA WHICH OF THE TWO WAS TAKEN.

I CAME BACK TO MARTIS'S HOME AND LAOS SMILED BEAUTIFULLY AT ME.

THEN THE SERVANT CAME WITH AN INVITATION FOR LAOS AND ME TO GO TO THE PALACE OF THE TWO-HEADED GOD.

HE WANTED US TO APPEAR BEFORE HIM AT ONCE.

BUT MARTIS ASSURED US THAT THIS WAS ONLY IN ANSWER TO OUR REQUEST OF MARRIAGE.

I HOPE I WILL AWAKEN FROM THIS NON SENSICAL INCONGRUITY.

THERE WAS CONFLICT IN KAL'S DESIRE, FOR AS A SOUL I BEGAN TO UNDERSTAND, BUT IF LAOS AND I HAD THE SAME LEVEL OF UNDERSTANDING, WE COULD **CONTROL VIBRATIONS** AND **READ ONE ANOTHER'S THOUGHTS.**

64

MARTIS DROVE US TO THE PALACE, PAST THE TEAMING CROWD OF PILGRIMS. WE REACHED THE PALACE OF LIGHT WITHIN SECONDS AND MARTIS LEFT US THERE BEFORE THE GATES.

WE WERE MET BY A SUKHSHAMIAN WHO ALMOST AMUSED US DESPITE OUR SERIOUSNESS.

AS WE FOLLOWED HIM, IT CAME TO MY MIND THAT MASTERY OF ALL SITUATIONS DEPENDED UPON UNDERSTANDING.

PERCEPTION IS THE MASTER OF SPACE AND, EQUALLY, ACTION IS THE MASTER OF TIME.

A SET OF DOORS OPENED BEFORE I COULD CONSIDER THAT POINT.

WE WERE LED INTO THE ROOM AND THE GUARD FLUNG HIMSELF ON HIS KNEES BEFORE THE TWO-HEADED GOD SEATED UPON HIS GOLDEN THRONE.

THE PRIEST PUSHED BOTH OF US ON THE RUG TO OFFER OUR RESPECT TO THEIR MIGHTY GOD.

THE ANGRY COUNTENANCE STARED AT US WITH ITS HORRID EYE.

YOU LITTLE PEOPLE OF MY KINGDOM CAME TO RECEIVE BLESSINGS FROM ME, THE GREAT KAL, BUT YOU MUST EARN THE REWARD BY GIVING SOMETHING IN RETURN!

65

HIS HANDSOME FACE CAME FORWARD, SMILING, TO GIVE HIS BLESSING TO OUR MARRIAGE, AND I ASKED WHAT HE WANTED OF US.

HIS UGLY FACE SPRANG FORWARD. IT TERRIFIED US AND THIS MADE HIM LEER JOYFULLY.

KAL SPOKE AND HIS WORDS WERE LIKE WORD PICTURES WHICH HAD GREATER MEANING, WE BECAME SUBMISSIVE UNDER HIS IRRATIONAL WHIMS.

KAL COMMANDED US TO COMPEL SHARIR AND THE OTHERS TO SURRENDER. AND UNDER THE CIRCUMSTANCES, I BECAME A SERVILE FLATTERER ONLY TO AVOID HIS ANGER AND WRATH.

SHOULD I SUCCEED, MARRIAGE TO LAOS WOULD BE MY REWARD. FAILURE, HOWEVER, WOULD MEAN MY DESTRUCTION IN THE HANDS OF THE **TALONS OF TIME.**

THE WHOLE SCENE SEEMED LIKE A MOVIE WE WERE WATCHING INSTEAD OF PARTICIPATING IN.

A FLYING CAR WAS ORDERED TO FLY US TO DHIRADA.

THE CAR ARRIVED AT THE DOCK AND I HARDLY NOTICED WHAT WAS HAPPENING AROUND ME.

I WAS THINKING OF THE MISSION BEFORE US, BUT MY MIND WAS SPLIT BETWEEN MY LOYALTY TO SHARIR AND MY PROMISE TO KAL.

MY THOUGHTS WERE DROWNING IN A MAZE OF TURBULENCE.

WE SAILED ACROSS THE LAKE TO DHIRADA'S HOME ON TOP OF A STEEP BLUFF, BUT AT FIRST NO ONE ANSWERED OUR CALL. THEN DHIRADA OPENED THE DOOR AND HAPPILY GREETED US.

IN FRONT OF MY FRIENDS, CONFLICT TORE ME. I TRIED TO WORK OUT IN MY MIND WHAT TO SAY TO SHARIR.

SHARIR KNEW WHAT I WAS THINKING AND SAID THAT OUR MISSION TO MAKE HIM SURRENDER HAD FAILED, AND THAT LAOS WAS AGAIN UNDER THE CONTROL OF KAL. I ARGUED ABOUT KAL'S PROMISE TO FREE ALL OF US ONCE I FULFILLED THE MISSION.

BE CALM AND SIT. WE MUST PROJECT OURSELVES TO THE VILLAGE OF TRETA.

FROM THERE WE MAKE OUR WAY THROUGH THE VALLEY TO THE BORDER.

BUT TABA AND EZAN'S DEATHS SHOCKED ME. LAOS URGED ME TO LEAVE AT ONCE, BUT SHARIR HALTED HER AND PUT HER UNDER HYPNOSIS. THEN THE VIEW SCREEN BLINKED AS INVADERS CLOSED IN ON US.

WHAT ABOUT LAOS? WILL SHE BE TAKEN WITH US?

SHARIR COULD NOT PROMISE A SAFE PASSAGE FOR LAOS TO EARTH. HE BLAMED ME FOR MY LACK OF TRAINING.

DHIRADA URGED ALL OF US TO START VISUALIZING THE VILLAGE OF TRETA, BUT THE IMAGE OF LAOS FILLED MY MIND.

67

A STRANGE THOUGHT RAN THROUGH MY MIND: IF CURVES ARE MORE GRACEFUL THAN BROKEN LINES, THEN A CURVED LINE COULD CHANGE ITS DIRECTION AT ANY MOMENT.

EVERY LINE COULD BE INDICATED BY THE LINE IT FOLLOWS.

AND EASY UNDERSTANDING OF MOTION COULD BE TRANSFORMED INTO MASTERING TIME AND HOLDING THE FUTURE IN THE PRESENT.

THIS WOULD INVOLVE RHYTHM IN MOTION.

REGULARITY OF RHYTHM ESTABLISHES COMMUNICATION BETWEEN THE INDIVIDUAL AND THE FORCES OF NATURE.

THE VOICE CALLING INTERRUPTED MY THOUGHTS. I LEFT THE SHELTER AND CRAWLED ACROSS A FIELD OF ROCKS AND SHALES.

HERE EVERYTHING ENDED.

THERE WAS NOTHING HERE EXCEPT ROCKS WHOSE TOPS WERE LOST MANY MILES INTO THE HEAVENS.

I SAT DOWN AND BEGAN TO GET ANGRY AT THIS NONSENSE.

71

THEN MY PEOPLE ARE UNDER MY CONTROL. THIS APPLIES TO ALL FORMS OF ARTS, ESPECIALLY MUSIC. IT HYPNOTIZES, AND UNDER THIS SPELL 'I TAKE CHARGE.

'MUSIC STEALS AWAY THEIR ATTENTION FROM TIME, AND BECAUSE OF THIS, ONLY DURATION EXISTS. EXISTENCE CAN BE DESTROYED BUT DURATION CANNOT!' KAL SAID.

CREATIVE ACTION AND CONSERVATIVE ACTION ARE PERMANENT AND ONLY ACCIDENTALLY DIVISIBLE BECAUSE THEY ARE SUBJECT TO MOVEMENT. IF YOU CONSIDER EXISTENCE ITSELF IS INSTANTANEOUS.

SO, YOU SEE, THE CONTROL I USE ON MY SUKHSHAMIAN BEINGS DETERMINES THEIR DURATION.

KAL LIVES IN SUCCESSIVE DURATION WITH ALL HIS PARTS UNINTERRUPTEDLY FLOWING IN TIME.

HIS MIND IS UNLIMITED, THUS HIS EXISTENCE IS CONTINUOUS, FOUND ONLY IN MOVEMENT.

ON EARTH, MOVEMENT IS ONLY REAL WHEN LIFE CONTINUES THROUGH PERPETUAL CHANGE.

MOVEMENT CONTAINS PAST, PRESENT, AND FUTURE.

IT DOES NOT KNOW PAUSE OR REST. CHANGE SHOWS WHAT BELONGS TO TIME. IT IS THE MEANS UPON WHICH THE TWO POLES OF TIME WORK: THE BEGINNING AND ENDING.

MOVEMENT IS DIVIDED INTO SEVERAL SPECIES WHICH ARE DETERMINED BY THE FINAL END, OR GOAL. THE THREE KINDS OF REALITY IN THE FINAL END OF MOVEMENT ARE PLACE, QUANTITY, AND QUALITY.

PLACE MOVEMENT IS THAT LOCAL MOVEMENT FROM ONE PLACE TO ANOTHER.

QUALITATIVE MOVEMENT IS THE PASSING FROM ONE QUALITY TO ANOTHER AND THE QUANTITATIVE MOVEMENT IS THE PROGRESSIVE INCREASE OR DECREASE IN THE MASS OF BEING.

74

FROM CONTINUOUS MOVEMENT, KAL GIVES REAL LIFE TO TIME AND ALLOWS EARTH LOCAL MOVEMENT. EARTH TIME IS A DURATION WHICH WE DIVIDE AS DAYS, MONTHS, AND YEARS.

THIS DURATION POSSESSES TRUE UNITY, BECAUSE IN IT WE COULD SEE THE CONCRETE MOVEMENT OF THE ZODIAC AROUND THE PLANETS.

BUT THIS IS ONLY A RELATIVE MEASURE OF CONCRETE TIME BY IMPERFECT BEINGS.

THE MATERIAL SUBSTANCE OF SUKSHAM IS NOT LIMITED BY TIME, HENCE THEY ENJOY A PERMANENT STABLE PRESENT.

WE ARE THE HIGHEST OF ALL WORLDS, AND I, KAL NIRANJAN, AM THE KING OF EVERY GALAXY, UNIVERSE, AND WORLD!

THE DULL VOICE OF KAL THUNDERED INTO LAUGHTER THAT ECHOED THROUGH THE MOUNTAINS AND ROLLED AGAINST THE GORGES. I SHRANK BACK AND SPED AWAY AS FAST AS I COULD.

RUN! EARTHLING RUN, FOR THE SWORD OF DAIMYO WILL CUT YOU AT ANY MOMENT, HA HA HA!

I FLED, UNAWARE I WAS MOVING THROUGH ATMOSPHERE, RAVINES, RAINSTORMS, GALES, THROUGH DEEP GORGES AND OVER SHARP-FANGED MOUNTAINS.

NO ONE IS IN PURSUIT. BUT THE GUARDS CAN SPEED THROUGH THE AIR FASTER THAN ONE COULD IMAGINE!

I WAS PUZZLED BUT NOT FOR LONG, FOR LAOS FOLLOWED ME. I DOUBTED HER LOYALTY, BUT UPON READING MY MIND SHE SAID SHARIR HAD FREED HER FROM KAL'S CONTROL AND NOW SHE COULD GO WHERE EVER SHE WANTED.

I ASKED HER ABOUT THE SWORD OF DAIMYO, AND GAZED AT HER FACE.

IT'S AN ANCIENT SWORD USED BY ONE OF THE GREATEST WARRIORS OF THE TEMPLE OF KAL CALLED, DAIMYO!

75

DAIMYO'S MAGICAL SWORD DEFEATED THE ENEMIES OF SUKSHAM IN HIS DAYS.

KAL HAS USED IT WHENEVER HE WANTS TO DESTROY SOMEONE WITH HIS OWN HANDS.

THIS TIME HE FAILED BECAUSE I STOPPED HIM.

YOU? HOW COULD YOU STOP KAL?

HER FACE WAS SOLEMN AND DIGNIFIED.

LAOS REVEALED THAT SHARIR TOOK AWAY KAL'S CONTROL OVER HER AND WORKED THROUGH HER TO HELP ALL HE COULD.

I STOOD THERE AND THOUGHT ABOUT IT.

SHARIR, A MAGICAL BEING, COULD NOT BE LIMITED BY TIME AND SPACE. AND BECAUSE HE LIVES IN THE IMMORTAL NOWNESS OF THE SOUL,

HE COULD MAKE THINGS HAPPEN AT THE TWINKLING OF AN EYE.

LAOS ERASED MY DOUBTS, ASSURING ME THAT SHARIR WOULD DEFEAT THE KAL.

WE LEFT FOR THE VILLAGE OF TRETA AND CAUTIOUSLY WATCHED FOR KAL AND HIS SWORD.

THE SNOWY PEAKS GLITTERED IN THE SUNLIGHT, BUT THE MAGNIFICENT VIEW POINTED ME TO THE PROBLEM OF DURATION.

LAOS LED ME TO IMPASSABLE MOUNTAINS OVER GLACIERS AND SNOWS, THROUGH FIELDS OF WILD FLOWERS AND GORGES, FINALLY COMING DOWN THROUGH MIRRORED FIELDS.

I DIDN'T KNOW WHAT TO DO BUT LAOS SUGGESTED WE GO DOWN TO THE VILLAGE TO ASK ABOUT SHARIR AND HIS COMPANIONS THROUGH THE VILLAGE CHIEFTAIN.

THAT MAY BE THE BEST PLAN FOR US.

TIME WAS NO LONGER THE SWIFTEST OF THE GODS, KNOWN BY ITS FLIGHT ACROSS SPACE. IT WAS THE REFLECTION OF SPACE.

SINCE I WAS NOT IN THE BODY, I WAS ELSEWHERE.

I WISHED WE HAD THE DIARY WHICH MIGHT GIVE US THE KEY TO TIME THAT COULD GIVE THE SECRET OF ESCAPING THIS HORRID WORLD.

TO BE ELSEWHERE IN THIS STRANGE LAND MEANT ONE COULD BE WHERE ONE WISHES TO BE.

SUDDENLY, I THOUGHT OF THE IDEA OF ENTERING THE PALACE OF LIGHT TO GET THE DIARY OF JOHN SKALLY.

LAOS DID NOT LIKE THIS, BUT ONCE MORE I PUT MY MIND TO WORK.

I CONVINCED LAOS WITH THIS IDEA.

FOR HOURS, WE SKIRTED THE RIDGE AND CAME OUT OF THE CAVE, THEN THROUGH A TUNNEL LEADING TO THE PALACE OF LIGHT.

77

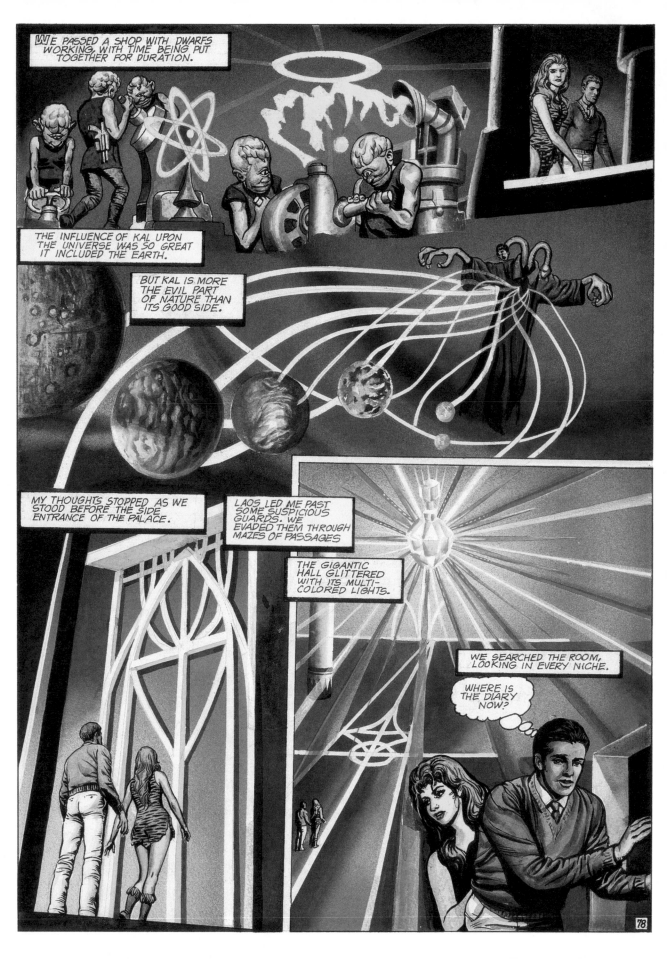

WE PASSED A SHOP WITH DWARFS WORKING, WITH TIME BEING PUT TOGETHER FOR DURATION.

THE INFLUENCE OF KAL UPON THE UNIVERSE WAS SO GREAT IT INCLUDED THE EARTH.

BUT KAL IS MORE THE EVIL PART OF NATURE THAN ITS GOOD SIDE.

MY THOUGHTS STOPPED AS WE STOOD BEFORE THE SIDE ENTRANCE OF THE PALACE.

LAOS LED ME PAST SOME SUSPICIOUS GUARDS. WE EVADED THEM THROUGH MAZES OF PASSAGES

THE GIGANTIC HALL GLITTERED WITH ITS MULTI-COLORED LIGHTS.

WE SEARCHED THE ROOM, LOOKING IN EVERY NICHE.

WHERE IS THE DIARY NOW?

78

LAOS WAS FOLLOWING ME HELPLESSLY WHEN FOOTSTEPS CAME FROM THE CORRIDOR AND ALARMED US.

I PULLED HER BEHIND THE THICK CURTAINS TO HIDE UNTIL THE SOLDIER ENDED THE SEARCH.

THE NET BECAME TOO THICK FOR US, AND THE FEAR OF BEING CAUGHT FRIGHTENED LAOS.

SHE MENTIONED THE THRONE, WHICH REMINDED ME OF A NICHE WHERE THE DIARY COULD BE ALONE AND UNGUARDED.

LEAD ME TO KAL'S COURT.

AS WE PASSED THE DAZZLING ROOM, MY BODY SEEMED TO BE TRANSFORMED INTO ONE BIG EYE ROLLING IN THE WORLD'S SOCKET.

THE VIEW OF THE THRONE FASCINATED US, AND WE STOOD THERE FORGETTING OUR MISSION.

AFTER SHAKING LAOS, I STARTED LOOKING FOR THE DIARY, BUT HER EYES WIDENED AT SOMETHING INSIDE THE NICHE.

I PUSHED HER ASIDE AND TOOK THE DIARY TO EXAMINE IT. IT WAS SKALLY'S DIARY AND THIS GOT ME EXCITED.

WE FOUND IT AT LAST! WE MUST FIND A SAFE PLACE TO READ IT!

79

WE SNEAKED THROUGH A SMALL DOOR AND PASSED THE HEAVILY GUARDED ROOM.

WE RETRACED OUR STEPS THROUGH THE CORRIDORS THAT LED TO THE DARK TUNNEL.

WHEN WE CAME OUT OF IT, LAOS SIGHED WITH RELIEF. SHE LED THE WAY TO THE EDGE OF THE FOREST AND UP THE MOUNTAIN.

WE WALKED UNDER THE TREES AND FINALLY CAME TO A SMALL CAVE WHICH LAOS ENTERED.

LYING UNDER THE LEDGE, THE CAVE WAS WELL-HIDDEN YET HAD PLENTY OF LIGHT TO LET US READ THE DIARY.

I STARTED READING THE BOOK.

BECAUSE THERE IS NO FIXED AND UNIFORM TIME, THE CONCEPT OF KEEPING ONE'S ATTENTION ON

EVOLUTION LOSES ALL MEANING. ITS CHANGING NATURE BELONGS ONLY TO THE WORLD OF APPEARANCE AND IS NOT A PART OF REALITY.

REALITY IS PERMANENT, AND TIME IS LOST IN AN ALL-INCLUSIVE HARMONY.

80

OUR BIASED BELIEF IN THE VARIABILITY OF TIME IS THE ONLY POWER TIME HAS OVER US.

THIS IS BECAUSE THE TIME MAKERS MADE US BELIEVE THIS WAY.

THE BEGINNING AND END OF OBJECTIVE WORLD SEPARATE FROM THE MIND DOES NOT EXIST.

IN THE WORLD OF REALITY, WE TRANSCEND THE ILLUSION OF OBJECTIVE TIME AND THE ILLUSION OF BEING, A SEPARATE SELF OVER AGAINST A WORLD WHICH IS NOT SELF.

THERE IS NO OBJECTIVE WORLD SO THERE IS NO OBJECTIVE TIME. IF I DIE TODAY, TOMORROW DOES NOT EXIST. ALL THEORIES OF THE FUTURE AS EARTH PEOPLE KNOW IT CONTAIN AN OBVIOUS MISTAKE WHICH THE TIME MAKERS IMPLANTED INTO OUR MINDS.

THESE BELIEFS ARE OBVIOUS MISTAKES BASED ON THE USUAL UNDERSTANDING OF STANDARD TIME.

BUT WE ARE NOT LIVING IN THE REAL WORLD.

EACH OF US TAKES OUR WORLD AND TIME WITH US WHEN WE DIE, THEN WE CREATE FROM OUR DESIRES OUR NEW WORLD AND OUR NEW TIME IN OUR NEXT TEMPORARY WORLD.

THIS IS WHY WE ARE AWARE OF SUKHSHAM, THE AFTER WORLD OF ZAPFS.

82

THE LAWS OF TIME ARE ILLOGICAL LAWS.

TRUTH IS OUTSIDE EVERY BEFORE AND AFTER.

BUT THE QUESTION OF PREDICTING THE FUTURE FROM A COMPLETE KNOWLEDGE OF THE PAST DOES NOT ARISE. IT IS SELF-CONTRADICTING.

TO UNDERSTAND THEM WE SHOULD THINK RATIONALLY, NOT HINDERED BY PRECONCEIVED OR IMPLANTED FACTS.

THERE IS NO FIXED PAST.

BUT EACH PERSON HAS HIS OWN ASSURED PAST AND FUTURE.

WE CREATE THE STRUCTURE OF TIME BUT ARE TERRIFIED BY ITS SIZE.

THE UNIVERSE IS GREAT BUT CONSCIOUSNESS IS GREATER BECAUSE IT ALONE CAN GRASP SUCH A UNIVERSE.

EACH OBSERVER LIVES IN HIS OWN TIME BUT THE UNIVERSE KNOWS NO TIME HISTORY.

CREATION IS NOT WITHIN ABSOLUTE TIME.

IT IS IN EACH OBSERVER'S TIME. WE CAN OBSERVE IT IN SPACE AND TIME, BUT WE ARE NOT IN THEM.

IT IS THE SAME TODAY, YESTERDAY, AND FOREVER.

THIS IS THE KEY TO TIME. THE EVENT OF CREATION COULD BE PLACED PRIOR TO THE EXPERIENCE OF THE INDIVIDUAL, BUT NO MEANING COULD BE ATTACHED BY ASKING WHAT WAS PRIOR TO CREATION.

THERE ARE NO OBSERVERS TO EXPERIENCE CREATION AS A TEMPORAL SEQUENCE.

TALKING AND DOING THINGS PUT US INTO THE HABIT OF ASSUMING THE IMPORTANCE OF **TIME** AND SPACE COORDINATES.

TIME PRIOR TO THE CREATION OF EARTH IS WITHOUT ANY SIGNIFICANCE.

FOR INSTANCE, WE DATE A LETTER ACCORDING TO THE DAY, MONTH, AND YEAR AND THIS CONTINUES **UNTIL WE WAKE UP FROM OUR DREAM.**

DREAMTIME ALSO PUTS US IN AN AWKWARD POSITION.

THE HIGHER ACTIVITIES OF MIND SUCH AS **THOUGHT** AND **WILL** DO NOT EXHIBIT EARTHLY DURATION WHEN WE EXAMINE THEM.

TO CONQUER THESE ILLUSIONS, WE SHOULD COMPLETELY CHANGE OUR WAY OF THINKING AND ACQUIRE NEW HABITS OF THINKING OF THE SYSTEM AS A WHOLE. THIS WILL FREE US FROM THINGS THAT BIND US TO TIME.

WE CAN THEREFORE LIVE IN ETERNAL FREEDOM.

TIME IS CONNECTED WITH THE CHANGEABLE NATURE OF MASS, THE DIFFERENCE BETWEEN TRANSVERSAL MASS AND LONGITUDINAL MASS; INERT MASS, PONDEROUS MASS;

THE IDENTIFICATION OF MASS ENERGY;

THE QUESTION OF RELATIVITY AND THE DEFORMATION OF SPACE.

TO WORK WITHIN TIME YOU MUST START WITH ACTION OF FEELING FROM OUR FACULTY THAT COULD CHANGE THINGS...

SO WE PLACE OURSELVES AT ONCE IN THE MIDST OF EXTENDED IMAGES, AND IN THIS WORLD WE CAN PERCEIVE THE CENTERS OF LIFE'S CHARACTERISTICS.

A POWER CONFIRMED BY CONSCIOUSNESS FROM WHICH ALL ORGANIZED BODIES COME.

IN ORDER THAT ACTION MAY RADIATE FROM THESE CENTERS, THE INFLUENCES OF OTHER IMAGES MUST BE RECEIVED AND UTILIZED.

PURE PERCEPTION IS A PART OF THINGS.

IT IS ONE WITH THE NECESSARY MODIFICATIONS TO WHICH, DESPITE THE SURROUNDING IMAGES THAT INFLUENCE IT, THIS PRIMAL IMAGE DIRECTS ALL THINGS OF ITS BEING.

THIS IS ONE OF THE SECRETS OF TIME.

AS FOR EFFECTIVE SENSATION, IT DOES NOT COME SPONTANEOUSLY FROM THE DEPTH OF CONSCIOUSNESS BECAUSE IT BECOMES WEAKER IN SPACE.

85

THEREFORE, ALL QUESTIONS RELATING TO SUBJECT AND OBJECT, TO THEIR DIFFERENCE AND UNION SHOULD BE PUT IN TERMS OF TIME RATHER THAN SPACE.

THUS WE HAVE PAST IMAGES SURVIVING UNDER TWO DISTINCT FORMS:

FIRST, IN MOTOR MECHANISMS, AND SECOND, IN INDEPENDENT RECOLLECTION.

THE THEORY OF VISION IS, THEN, WHATEVER YOU PERCEIVE YOU CAN CONCEIVE.

THIS IS IN THE LIGHT OF THINKING AND LOOKING AT THE SCREEN OF TIME AND SPACE WITH THE INNER EYE, AND FORMING THE IDEAL IN YOUR LIFE.

THIS IS THE BEGINNING OF PROJECTION, THE OVERCOMING OF TIME AND SPACE.

AND SINCE THERE IS NO TIME BUT MEMORIES, THEN ONE HAS TO OVERCOME MEMORIES INSTEAD OF THE ELEMENT OF TIME.

THE FACULTY OF MENTAL PHOTOGRAPHY BELONGS TO THE SUBCONSCIOUS, AND AT THE SAME TIME THE FOUNDATION OF CONSCIOUS IMAGE.

86

TO OVERCOME TIME, ONE MUST PLACE HIMSELF IN THE CENTER OF HIS MENTAL PICTURE AND ACT AS THOUGH HE IS THE AUTHOR, ACTOR, AND DIRECTOR OF THE ACTION—WHICH HE REALLY IS.

THIS COLLAPSES SPACE AND BYPASSES ALL TIME, AND ONE WILL GAIN CONTACT WITH *REBAZAR TARZS* AND OTHER *ECK MASTERS.*

IT IS THE SECRET WHICH THE TIME MAKERS HAVE HIDDEN FROM THE PEOPLE OF THIS EARTH.

I COULD NOW UNDER-STAND MY PROBLEM. I NEEDED MY BODY, WHICH I LEFT IN *PAOSHAN.* IF I COULD PROJECT MYSELF AND LAOS TO THE WAY STATION WE COULD

POSSIBLY REACH EARTH FROM THERE.

BECAUSE *SUKHSHAM* AND EARTH WERE IN TWO DIFFERENT SYSTEMS OF TIME, IT WAS NOT POSSIBLE TO OPERATE IN BOTH WITH ONE OF THE OTHER BODIES. I SAT DOWN TO CON-CENTRATE. I HAD BEEN MISSING THE WHOLE TRICK BY LACK OF CON-CENTRATION IN THE RIGHT DIRECT-ION. THEN LAOS TIMIDLY ASKED,

WHAT DOES IT SAY, BELOVED?

IT SAYS THAT WE CAN ESCAPE FROM SUKHSHAM AND GO BACK TO THE EARTH WORLD. IT TELLS US HOW TO DO IT!

LAOS DOUBTED OUR ABILITY TO SUCCEED IN PROJECTION, AND HER OPPOSITION MADE ME ANGRY. SUDDENLY, IN THE HEAT OF OUR DISCUSSION, THE MOUNTAIN BEGAN TO SHAKE.

WHAT'S WRONG?

87

WE HEARD A HEAVY THUD, THE SOUND OF SOMETHING TEARING TREES AND CRUSHING THEM LIKE MATCHSTICKS AGAINST THE SNOW.

THEN, A GIGANTIC MONSTER APPEARED AGAINST THE DARKENED SKY. IT WAS THE TALONS OF TIME.

WE ESCAPED THE HUGE BOULDERS CRASHING DOWN THE MOUNTAIN.

THE MONSTER KEPT STALKING US.

I TUCKED THE MANUSCRIPT INSIDE THE POCKET OF MY SHIRT AS WE STRUGGLED TO SAVE OUR LIVES, BUT OUR ATTEMPT

WAS HOPELESS. FOR NOW THE MONSTER STOOD BEFORE US, WAITING TO DEVOUR US.

WE HAD TO ESCAPE BUT WHERE? I REMEMBERED JOHN SKALLY'S DIARY WHICH STATED: **TO PERCEIVE IS TO CONCEIVE.**

I WISHED HARD FOR A PLACE TO HIDE, DESPITE THE SHAKING STEPS OF THE APPROACHING MONSTER.

88

SUDDENLY, WE WERE IN A CAVERN.

LAOS AND I STRUGGLED AGAINST THE GALE AND THE WHIPPING WINDS OF THE WORLD.

BELOW US WAS A GRAY BLANKET OF CLOUDS, AND ABOVE US CLOUDS OF SILVER STRETCHED ACROSS THE HEAVENS.

ROCKS SHEARED BY WINDS AND PEAKS THAT HIDE THEIR SUMMIT IN HEAVENS, AND MOUNTAINS WITH THEIR BASES FADING SEVERAL DOZEN MILES BELOW GREETED US.

LAOS SAID THE **TALONS OF TIME** WAS ONLY THE **KAL** IN ONE OF HIS ROLES. I COULD NOT BELIEVE WE WERE SO HIGH AND WERE WE SAFE FROM THE MONSTER? THEN MOUNT AKNOK APPEARED, ONLY...

TO DISAPPEAR AGAIN IN THE MIST.

LAOS SUGGESTED WE GIVE UP THE DIARY, WHICH I RESENTED FURIOUSLY.

SHE GAVE UP HER NAGGING AND AGREED TO COOPERATE. FINALLY WE SAT DOWN ON THE COLD FLOOR OF THE CAVE TO CONCENTRATE.

89

SOMETHING DARK AGAINST THE GLISTENING LIGHT ATTRACTED ME.

AND SIGHTED THE SHREDDED FIGURE OF A WOMAN COMPLETELY DESTROYED. MY SORROW WAS OVERWHELMING, I LOST ALL DESIRE TO SURVIVE.

I PLUMMETED DOWN THROUGH THIS LONELY SPACE AND SAW A DARK SPOT ON THE SNOW.

LAOS WAS GONE. I HAD LOST MY WHOLE WORLD.

IT DIDN'T MATTER TO ME NOW WHAT WOULD HAPPEN TO EARTH, TO THE MAGICIANS AND THEIR FRIENDS.

I COULD NOT IMAGINE LIVING WITHOUT HER.

SHE WAS ONLY AN ATOM NOW WITHOUT FEELING OR SENSATION.

I ROSE TO MY FEET, DETERMINED TO GO BACK TO EARTH TO BRING DESTRUCTION TO THIS DREADFUL REGION.

SHE HAD ALREADY PASSED INTO THE REGION OF COMPLETE DARKNESS AND UNCONSCIOUSNESS.

91

THIS PLACE WAS EMPTY, AND ITS WHITE MISTY SILENCE WAS DEAFENING AND GIGANTIC AS ITS SPACE.

I DIDN'T KNOW WHERE TO GO AND WHAT TO DO.

THEN **MOUNT AKNOK** APPEARED, SHIMMERING WITH ITS MAJESTIC VIEW.

THE AIR CHILLED.

BLACK CLOUDS FILLED THE END OF THE GORGE...

OVERFLOWED...

TUMBLED DOWN THE FLANK OF THE MOUNTAIN, **ONE** AFTER ANOTHER, OBLITERATING IT.

MOUNT AKNOK GLEAMED AT THE END OF THE GORGE, THEN MOVED AND DISAPPEARED.

A HUGE CLAWED HAND CAME OUT OF THE FOGGY SKY AS THOUGH READY TO SEIZE ME.

THE MOUNTAIN DEVELOPED INTO HUGE FEET, CRUSHING AND PULVERIZING THE PEAKS AND VALLEYS AND MOUNTAINS.

I SHRIEKED IN TERROR.

92

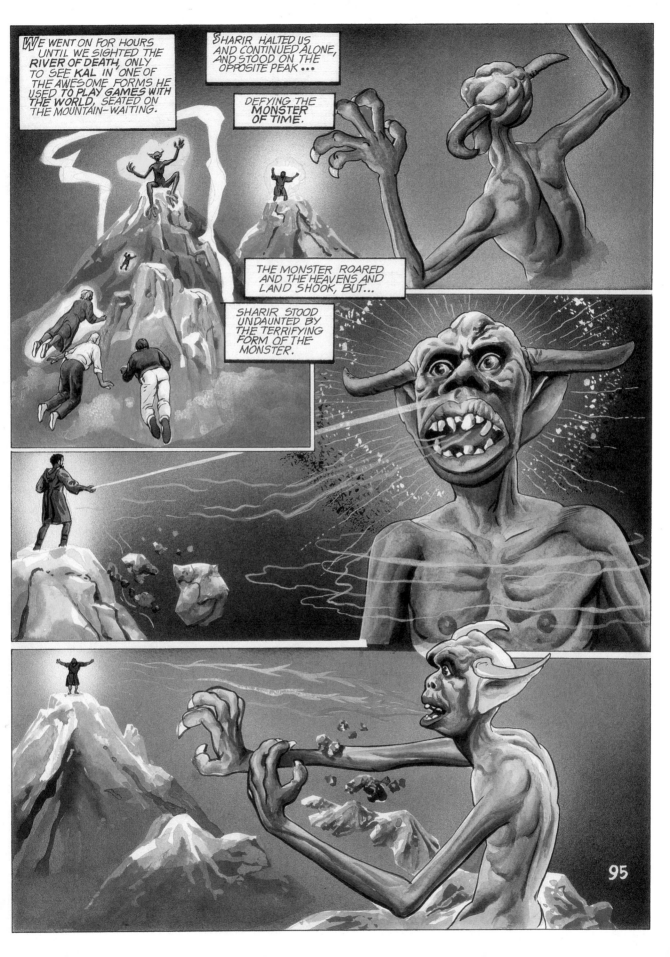

FOR FURTHER READING AND STUDY

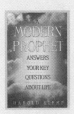

A Modern Prophet Answers Your Key Questions about Life
Harold Klemp

A pioneer of today's focus on "everyday spirituality" shows you how to experience and understand God's love in your life—anytime, anyplace. His answers to hundreds of questions help guide you to your own source of wisdom, peace, and deep inner joy.

The Tiger's Fang
Paul Twitchell

Visit the Sun and Moon Worlds. Discover the fabulous Mountain of Light. Author Paul Twitchell was the modern-day founder of Eckankar. His teacher, Rebazar Tarzs, takes him on an incredible journey through vast worlds of Light and Sound. Uncover the secret of how you, too, can find your way home to God—and awaken as Soul to your spiritual destiny.

Our Spiritual Wake-Up Calls, Mahanta Transcripts, Book 15
Harold Klemp

When God calls, are you listening? Discover how God communicates through dreams, the people you meet, or even a newspaper comic strip. Learn how you are in the grasp of divine love every moment of every day. The Mahanta Transcripts are highlights from Harold Klemp's worldwide speaking tours.

The Spiritual Exercises of ECK
Harold Klemp

This book is a staircase with 131 steps. It's a special staircase, because you don't have to climb all the steps to get to the top. Each step is a spiritual exercise, a way to help you explore your inner worlds. And what awaits you at the top? The doorway to spiritual freedom, self-mastery, wisdom, and love.

Available at your local bookstore. If unavailable, call (612) 544-0066. Or write: ECKANKAR, P.O. Box 27300, Minneapolis, MN 55427 U.S.A.

ABOUT THE AUTHOR

When Paul Twitchell made Eckankar known to the modern world in 1965, he separated spiritual truths from the cultural trappings which had surrounded them. Average people could begin to experience the Light and Sound of God while still living a happy, steady, and productive life.

Paul Twitchell was born in Kentucky in the early part of this century and served in the U.S. Navy during the Second World War.

A seeker from an early age, he was introduced to a group of spiritual Masters who would change the course of his life. These were the Vairagi ECK Masters. While they trained Paul to become the Living ECK Master, he explored a wide range of spiritual traditions under different teachers. The high teachings of ECK had been scattered to the four corners of the world. Paul gathered these golden teachings of Light and Sound and made them readily available to us.

It was these God experiences he chronicled in his book *The Tiger's Fang.* Paul Twitchell eventually joined the Vairagi Order and was given the task of bringing Eckankar to the world. He became the Living ECK Master.

By 1965, Paul was giving Soul Travel workshops in California and offering discourses on the teachings of Eckankar. A community of ECKists began to grow. In 1970, Eckankar was established as a nonprofit religious organization. Paul Twitchell died in 1971, but not before he initiated many into the ECK teachings.

The present Living ECK Master is Sri Harold Klemp. He continues in his footsteps, giving new life to the age-old spiritual teachings of ECK.